what could have been

LAKE LENORA
BOOK 1

HEATHER GUERRE

author's note

What Could Have Been touches on topics that may be difficult for some readers, including: child abuse (past, off-page, emotional not physical), neurodivergence struggles (ADHD), alcoholism and unintentional self-medication (related to undiagnosed neurodivergence), and loneliness and social isolation. This story also contains explicit depictions of sexual intimacy.

before

THE STUDENT PARKING lot was empty, a field of open pavement. It was way better for skating than the narrow alley behind the post office. It wouldn't be long before one of the school custodians chased Noah and the others away but, until then, they'd take advantage.

For now, the only thing in the world was the board beneath Noah's feet and his balance upon it. He glided up to the edge of the lot, pushing himself faster and faster, gaining enough speed to carry his momentum as he ollied up onto the curb. He rode the grind along the rough cement for longer than he expected to. He was distantly aware of his friends cheering him, but when he pressed his weight back and came off the curb, the first person he saw when he looked up was Ashlyn Vandale, standing on the sidewalk, watching him.

Blonde, athletic, smart, pretty, *perfect* Ashlyn. Her perfection irritated him, but he wasn't so thick that he couldn't recognize when he had a crush. An irritating crush. But, still.

Ashlyn was dressed in sports gear—short little soccer shorts with long, striped socks pulled up over her knees. Didn't she know what she looked like, walking around like that? She might be gorgeous, but Noah'd never gotten the impression that she cared about attracting boys' attention. If anything, his entire gender seemed to annoy her. Still, she couldn't be totally oblivious.

He lifted his gaze to meet hers, unable to bite back his smile. "Nice socks."

She didn't react to the jibe, except to furrow her brow slightly. She seemed like she was trying to figure out if he was insulting her or not. He wasn't really sure what he was doing. He never knew what he was doing around Ashlyn Vandale.

Her soft brown eyes traveled over him, taking in his oversized Gorillaz t-shirt, baggy jeans, and dirty DC sneakers. Her focus made him feel squirrelly. He had to force himself to stand still, to keep the confident smirk on his face. He knew his clothes were grubby and that he smelled like pot. He'd just smoked a bowl with Tyler Kemp and Nate Vogel. Ashlyn probably smelled like fresh-cut grass and girl sweat. Which undoubtedly smelled amazing.

"Why do you smell like a skunk?" Ashlyn finally asked, brow still furrowed, doe-like eyes pinning him in place.

He forced himself to grin wider. "A *skunk*, Ash? Aw. Your naivety is cute."

Her furrowed brow turned into a scowl. "'Naivety'? Wow. Don't strain your brain too hard with so many syllables."

Instantly, his smile dropped. He couldn't fake it any longer. Of course she thought he was an idiot. Why wouldn't she? Everyone else did.

"Thanks for your concern, Princess." It was an old

insult, and completely lame, but it was the only one he had. Ashlyn and all her perfect little friends were called the "Princesses" by envious, burnout losers like Noah.

"Don't call me—" she cut herself off as her gaze snapped away from him.

He followed her line of sight to the parking lot entrance, where a shiny Crown Victoria was pulling in. That would be Judy Vandale, Ashlyn's grandma, come to pick her perfect granddaughter up after her wholesome afternoon of high-achieving athletic activity.

"Bye, Noah," she said distractedly. The hostility completely left her voice and expression as she hurried away from him.

Didn't want her saintly grandma to see her associating with him?

He couldn't really blame her there.

one

"DID you hear Ashlyn Vandale is back in town?"

It'd been more than a decade since Noah had last seen Ashlyn Vandale, and she hadn't crossed his mind much since then, but hearing her name still sparked a frisson of irritation. His brother Wesley knew it, too, judging by the shit-eating smirk on his face. Noah couldn't give Wes the satisfaction of getting a rise out of him.

"There's a name I haven't heard in a long time," he replied neutrally.

Wes shrugged, turning his attention back to the grout float in his hand. "Her grandma died. Guess she's come back to settle the estate."

Noah snorted. "She left town the minute she graduated and never visited that poor old woman even once. But now that there's money on the table, she finally decides to show her face again?"

Wes's gaze lifted to Noah's. The smirk was back. "You sound a little bitter there, brother."

He shouldn't have been. It's not like Ashlyn Vandale was

a traumatic part of his life. She'd been more like a constant irritant. She was *perfect*. Not worshipful perfection, but rather, suspicious, too-good-to-be-true perfection. She'd been the valedictorian of their graduating class, varsity captain of the girls' volleyball and soccer teams, first violin in the school orchestra, editor-in-chief of the school news-paper, and had spent every Sunday in church.

Her parents had died when she was two, and she'd been raised by her grandmother. Noah might have felt bad about that if she hadn't milked that sob story for all it was worth—the sad little orphan bit really added to the adulation everyone heaped on her. On top of all that, the girl had been senselessly beautiful, which was just a waste, because in all the years Noah had known her, not a single person had ever thawed that perfect ice queen.

In contrast, Noah had been the constantly-high delin-quent burnout who'd only managed to graduate high school by the skin of his teeth. And he'd had no excuse. He came from a big, loving, supportive family. They weren't rich, but they weren't poor. Their parents had happily shuttled them to practices, paid for sports equipment and instruments, cheered them on no matter what their pursuits. Noah had had all the resources to match Ashlyn's perfection, and instead, he'd been her polar opposite.

In their small Northwoods town, at their small school, there was no avoiding her. When Noah was sentenced to community service at the food pantry after too many underage drinking citations, Ashlyn was there too—except she was a willing volunteer. When his parents found out he was failing trigonometry, he'd been forced into after-school tutoring—and guess who his tutor was. That's right. Ashlyn Vandale. When he was under the bleachers getting high, Ashlyn was on the field practicing penalty kicks. When he was bringing booze to high school parties, Ashlyn was giving everyone safe rides home.

She was better than Noah. He didn't deny it. But she'd known it too, and she never let him forget it.

At the end of their first tutoring session, when she'd figured out that he was failing not because he didn't understand the material, but simply because he wasn't doing the homework, she looked at him like he was repulsive. *"You're purposely failing? What the hell, Noah?"*

She wasn't wrong to be appalled. But that didn't mean all her sneers and insults and dirty looks had been justified. Didn't mean that her self-righteous condemnation hadn't cut right through him. He wasn't a fuck-up because he'd wanted to be. He was a fuck-up because his brain wasn't screwed in right.

After high school, Ashlyn went off to Madison on a scholarship, while Noah spent the next several years sinking even deeper into the pit of his own self-destructiveness. His high-school outlets of alcohol and weed began morphing into more dangerous vices. His brothers and sister all went off to college while he floundered in their little hometown, living with a bunch of other burnouts, working shitty temp construction jobs, barely getting by.

Salvation came in the form he'd have least expected. He'd been twenty-three and working a roofing job when the foreman, Steve Kubiczek, pulled him aside. Like every job, he was constantly turning up late and he'd figured Steve was finally giving him the boot. Instead, Steve told Noah that he reminded him of his nephew—a good kid, a smart kid, but kind of a screw-up. Turned out Steve's nephew had ADHD and once the kid got on a decent treatment plan, things started coming together for him.

It seemed like too much to hope that all Noah's failures

were symptoms of a manageable condition, and not just intrinsic to who he was as a person. But, after being badgered by Steve, he went to the doctor. And after jumping through all the hoops, he got a diagnosis—ADHD, just like Steve's nephew. Noah and his doctor spent nearly a year trying to settle on the right medication and dosage, and in the midst of that, he joined a sobriety group and went to therapy to learn better coping mechanisms, and by the time he hit twenty-four, life had gotten so much better.

And now, here he was, thirty-four years old, clean and sober, the successful owner of his own contracting business, a contributing member of society, and... still angry at Ashlyn Fucking Vandale for making him feel like such a useless piece of shit when he was a teenager.

To be fair, it's not like this was some kind of ancient blood feud that he couldn't stop obsessing over. In fact, since she'd left Lenora, Ashlyn Vandale rarely crossed his mind. But now she was back and the insecure resentment that he thought he'd grown out of years ago was suddenly burning in his chest again.

"You okay?"

He glanced over and saw Wes watching him with a frown, all of his smirky amusement gone.

"Fine," Noah said flatly. "Are we going to finish this tile today or not?"

After securing the financing and buying a portion of the decrepit ruins of the Lake Lenora Resort—once owned by their grandparents, but lost to a bad business partnership when they were little kids—Wes had hired Noah to bring it back to habitability. Noah and his crew did the majority of the labor, but Wes rolled up his sleeves and pitched in when he had time off from his day job.

Noah's crew had gone home for the night, and now it

was just him and his brother, finishing the tile floor in the last bathroom in the main lodge. Wes looked at the remaining stretch of floor—maybe an hour or two of work —then at his watch. "Yeah, let's get it done. Want to swing by the Wooden Nickel after this?"

"I'm tired, Wes."

"It's seven o'clock on a Friday, old man."

"You're two years older than me, *older* man."

"Yeah, but I act my age. You act like you're eighty."

He wasn't entirely wrong. Since getting his company off the ground, Noah spent most of his time working, and when he wasn't working, he was too tired to do anything but sit at home. He'd been ducking out of invites for too long.

"If you go out, you know Aiden will, too," Wes pressed.

Aiden, two years younger, was even more reclusive than Noah. He tended to only go out if Noah was there too. Aiden had never said it in so many words, but Noah suspected it was because he was the only one of their brothers who didn't give him constant shit for being a homebody who still lived with Mom and Dad.

Noah sighed. "Alright. Just one drink." For him, a drink meant diet coke with a lime twist. Some recovered alcoholics couldn't set foot in a bar—couldn't even stand to look at a beer. Noah was fine being around alcohol, watching other people imbibe, he just didn't let himself partake anymore. So he stuck to soda while others were letting loose, and counted his lucky stars that he wasn't who he used to be.

two

ASHLYN VANDALE STOOD outside the house where she grew up, clutching the key in one sweaty fist, unable to make herself step up onto the front porch. She hadn't seen the little white bungalow in over a decade, and she'd been hoping to never see it again. But of course, Grandma went and left Ashlyn her entire estate—saddling her with a chaotic jumble of debts and assets that she hadn't bothered to account for in at least two decades. Grandma had taken care of her finances about as well as she'd taken care of her only grandchild, and now Ashlyn was frantically trying to piece it all together before the IRS came down on her like the smiting hand of an angry god.

She took another breath, pushing away the anxiety that was making her hands sweat and her shoulders hunch.

She's gone. They're both gone. It's just an empty house. You're an adult and you're in control of your life now. There's nothing to be afraid of.

As true as all that was, it didn't make the fear go away. But she hadn't escaped her grandma's clutches by letting fear paralyze her. She hauled in one more breath, adjusted her grip on her duffel bag, and stepped up onto the porch.

"Hey, that house is empty," somebody called from behind her.

Ashlyn looked over her shoulder to see a woman on the sidewalk, holding the leash of a dog that looked more like a polar bear.

"Oh, I know. I… I guess I own it now?"

The woman tilted her head, squinting at her. "Ashlyn Vandale?"

Ashlyn turned to face her. "Yeah. You are…?"

"Rose Reznik. I was a year below you in school. We were both on the soccer team."

"Rose!" She spun around, grateful for the reprieve from the house, and trotted over to where her old friend stood on the sidewalk. "Of course I remember you. I didn't recognize you at first. You look so different—your hair! And, you know, your clothes—"

Rose held out her arms, glancing down at herself. She was wearing a burgundy colored parka with black jeans, a teal shirt with a white screenprint of a band name Ashlyn vaguely recognized, and a pair of rose-patterned Dr. Martens that appeared to be hand-painted.

"You're not used to seeing me in color," Rose said with a smile.

In high school, she'd been an intimidatingly cool emo kid. Her clothes had been black, her hair black, her eye make-up super black. Now her long, wavy hair was a deep, vivid burgundy that made her pale gray eyes stand out like glittering smoke. Her once ultra-skinny brows were now thick and perfectly arched and her eyes were softly lined. In high school, she'd had her tongue and her eyebrow and her lip pierced, but now those were gone and instead she had only a delicate silver septum piercing.

"Well, anyways, you look great."

"You too," she said, giving Ashlyn a once over.

Ashlyn hadn't changed all that much. She still had boring dishwater blonde hair, brown eyes, pale skin. She had a few more freckles than she'd had in high school, and her face wasn't as youthfully round as it had once been. But she'd never had a distinctive style, and she still didn't. She was wearing a plain navy peacoat over an ordinary gray sweater and jeans, with a red knit cap pulled over her hair.

"God, I can't believe how long it's been," Rose said. "Where have you been? What have you been up to?"

"I've been in Chicago for a while now. I'm an accountant."

"Oh, right—I think your grandma told my mom about that a few years ago. You're a CPA, right?"

Ashlyn was surprised to learn that Grandma talked about her to other people. After she left, Grandma had told her never to darken her doorstep again. Then again, she wasn't totally shocked. Even when she was berating Ashlyn at home for every minuscule failure, Grandma had loved to crow about her granddaughter's successes to all her church friends—and take credit for them.

"Uh, yeah. I work for a firm that does external audits of other companies." She tried not to wince as she explained. She didn't even care about her job, why would other people?

"Awesome. What else you been up to? Married? Kids?"

"No and no," she said, making her voice light.

"Yeah, me neither. Too much hassle, right?"

Ashlyn laughed in agreement, reaching down to pet the

monstrously fluffy beast who was snuffling at her coat. "And who's this guy?"

"Meet Nimbus. I'm pretty sure he's a dog."

Nimbus pranced excitedly as Ashlyn rubbed his ears, leaning his massive body against her legs and nearly knocking her over.

"So how long are you in town?" Rose asked. "Got time to catch up? I'm meeting some friends at The Wooden Nickel in an hour. You remember Dia Vang and Laila Turner?"

"Yeah, of course I remember them." Dia and Ashlyn had been in orchestra together, and Laila's family belonged to the same parish as Ashlyn's grandma.

"You should come by, then. I'm sure they'd like to see you. "

Ashlyn had been dreading returning to Lenora to get Grandma's house cleaned out, but seeing an old friend warmed her in a way that she hadn't felt in a long time. Rose was familiar and comfortable without being oppressive and smothering as her grandma had always been.

"Yeah, that sounds good actually."

Rose hugged her, and she almost dropped her bag in surprise. She couldn't remember the last time somebody had hugged her. It took conscious effort not to hold onto Rose for way too long.

"See you in a little bit." Rose broke away, waved, and continued on her walk with Nimbus.

Ashlyn turned back to Grandma's house. Time to face the music. She marched up to the porch, unlocked the door, and let herself in.

She flicked on the hall light and immediately gagged. The place was even worse than she'd anticipated. It reeked of cat urine and rotten garbage. Hoarded junk overflowed the front room and spilled into the entryway. A thick rind of dust covered every surface. As she stepped deeper into the chaos, the gouged, sticky linoleum flexed alarmingly beneath her feet.

This wasn't going to be a quick weekend of cleaning before getting the house listed to sell. This was several weeks of work—and likely more, if the sagging floor was any indication of the structural integrity.

Grandma was gone, but the suffocating anxiety of her presence wrapped around Ashlyn with familiar unease. She stood in the middle of all the ruin, swamped with decades-old revulsion. She couldn't stay here. Even if it didn't smell like absolute hell, she still wouldn't have been able to bear it.

She strode back out of the house, not even bothering to lock the door. If somebody wanted to rob the place, they'd only be doing her a favor. She threw her bag back into her car, got in, and pulled away from the curb. She'd get a hotel room. She'd pay somebody to empty out the house, and she'd pay somebody else to do the necessary repairs. And then she'd sell that haunted hovel, leave Lenora, and never look back.

three

THE NICKEL WAS SLAMMED, which was typical for a Friday night. Aiden had turned down their invite, so it was just Noah and Wes. They found two seats at the bar and Noah ordered his usual coke with a twist of lime, while Wes got a tap beer. They hadn't been there even five minutes when Noah felt somebody crash into him.

"*Oof!*" A woman in a red knit hat bounced off of his shoulder. His hand shot out reflexively, catching her by the arm, keeping her on her feet.

"You okay?" he asked.

"I'm alright, thanks," she said, pawing her long blonde hair out of her face. She straightened her hat, and when she looked up at him, his breath caught in his throat.

Ashlyn Vandale.

She was just as beautiful as she'd always been. More beautiful, actually. Her cheekbones were sharper than they'd been when she was a teenager, her jaw more angular. Golden freckles scattered across her cheeks and the bridge of her nose. Her mouth was still a rosy pout, her hair still as long and flaxen as a fairytale princess's. She looked back at him, aggravatingly perfect, without even a hint of recognition shining in those soft brown eyes.

"Sorry about that," she said as if she was speaking to a total stranger. "It's packed in here." Behind her, a crowd of jostling assholes laughed and shouted at each other, oblivious to the woman they'd nearly sent sprawling.

He couldn't seem to make himself speak. He just stared at her, feeling like an awkward seventeen-year-old in a grown man's body.

"Hey!" Wes leaned over, a broad smile on his face. "Not Ashlyn Vandale?"

She looked at him for a moment before recognition dawned, and a smile warmed her face. "Wesley Sorenson! No way. Hi!"

Wes pulled her in for a friendly hug that made Noah's stomach twist unpleasantly. Should he do the same? Would she want that? She seemed fine with Wes. But—

"How have you been?" she asked, pulling out of his hug. She looked at Noah and straightened. "Oh, I'm sorry. I'm Ashlyn Vandale. I grew up here." She held her hand out to shake.

Noah glanced down at it, then back up at her face. "I know who you are, Ashlyn," he said, forcing himself to sound amused instead of insulted.

Her gaze flickered uncertainly between Noah and Wes, settling back on Noah with zero recognition. "Well… you look like a Sorenson…" She considered him for a moment.

He raised his eyebrows.

"You're not Aiden," she said confidently.

He shook his head.

"James?" She guessed his twin's name, which wasn't so bad.

Another shake of his head.

Her eyes narrowed. "Lucas?" She guessed his youngest brother's name, and it got harder to keep his expression affable.

"Nope."

Her eyes widened. "No way. Not Noah."

"I knew you'd get there eventually."

"*Noah?*" She stared at him as if he were an alien. "But you—you look—"

To be fair, his appearance had changed quite a bit since high school. He was no longer a lanky beanpole dressed in oversized hoodies and baggy jeans. Fifteen years of working construction had added decent mass onto his frame, and he was wearing clothes that actually fit him. His hair was still coal black, though he kept it trimmed short now instead of letting it grow down to his shoulders, and it was beginning to thread with gray at the temples. The wispy mustache he'd been trying so hard to grow at seventeen had turned into a full-fledged beard. And most significantly, he didn't have perpetually glazed, red eyes anymore.

"Wow," she said, looking truly awed. "You look really different." She meant it as a compliment, but all he heard was, *Wow. You don't look like such a wasted loser anymore.*

"You look the same," he replied. "Except older."

Her smile faltered as if she wasn't sure if that was an insult or not. He hadn't consciously meant it that way, but the resentful, sullen teenager currently occupying his subconscious might not have been so benevolent.

"Time's been good to you," Wes told her, saving them all from Noah's lack of social grace. "Finally grew out of that baby face." He reached out as if to pinch her cheeks. Ashlyn ducked him, gasping with false outrage, but unable to hide a smile. That was Wesley Sorenson for you—aggressively charming in a way that few other men could pull off. If Noah had tried to pinch Ashlyn—or, hell, any woman— he'd have ended up with a black eye.

"Hands to yourself, Sorenson," she told his brother with an unconvincing glare.

"Sorry." Wes held his hands up innocently. "Let me buy you a drink to apologize."

"No, no, I forgive you. Besides, it's my turn to buy a round." She pointed to the far wall where Dia Vang, Rose Reznik, and Laila Turner were sitting together in a circular booth, talking and laughing.

"Girls' night?" Wes asked.

"Accidental reunion," Ashlyn answered. "I ran into Rose when I was at my grandma's house, and she invited me out."

"Right, I heard about your grandma," Wes said, sobering. "Sorry for your loss."

Ashlyn shrugged, her gaze darting away from them both. Noah didn't miss the flicker of distaste in her eyes. She might be all friendly and polite now, but apparently Ashlyn Vandale was still just as cold and self-important as she'd always been. Judy Vandale had taken in her orphaned granddaughter, given her a home, fed, clothed, and raised her—and all Ashlyn could offer was a shrug and barely-suppressed grimace. She hadn't even made it to the funeral.

"Well, we won't keep you," Noah said, turning back to the bar.

Wes cast him a questioning look but didn't argue. "It was nice seeing you, Ashlyn."

"You too. If I don't see either of you again before I leave town, well… have a nice life." She smiled politely and then moved down the bar to catch the bartender.

When she was out of earshot, Wes turned to glare at Noah. "What the hell is wrong with you?"

before

ASHLYN HAD BEEN SITTING at the library table for nearly fifteen minutes when Noah finally sauntered in. She watched surreptitiously as he went to the front desk for the signup sheet. He picked up the pen that was tied to the clipboard, bent his head to sign—and then immediately jerked his head up. He looked around the library until his gaze landed on Ashlyn. She sat with her arms crossed, affecting a look of displeasure.

Noah stalked over to her. "Of course I'm stuck with you." He rolled his eyes as he slumped into the chair next to her.

"I'm not thrilled about it either," Ashlyn lied. The truth was—she'd *chosen* Noah. Mr. Schettl let the tutoring volunteers choose from a list of kids who'd been assigned tutoring sessions. Ashlyn had seen Noah's name on the list and instantly written her name next to his without even thinking about it.

"Whatever." Noah opened his backpack, revealing a chaotic jumble of rumpled papers, beat-up notebooks, textbooks, and other odds and ends. He sorted through it for what felt like eons before he finally pulled out his Trigonometry textbook and a notebook that the front cover had been torn off of. The first page was covered in some kind of elaborate drawing. Ashlyn only got the sense of flapping wings and outstretched talons before he immediately flipped past it, shuffling through pages covered in all kinds of different stuff—math problems, paragraphs of writing, more drawings. Bits of things fell out of the pages as he flipped—old gum wrappers, a rubber band, flecks of what was probably marijuana. Finally, he found a blank page and slapped the notebook down on the table.

"I don't have my calculator," he said flatly.

Ashlyn slid her graphing calculator across the table to him. "You can use mine."

"Okay, fine. Now what, wise tutor?" he asked with impatient sarcasm.

"Okay, so we're supposed to do one through sixteen on page—"

"Yeah, I know." He flipped the page in the textbook, marked by a torn-off bit of notebook paper.

"Alright, so, why don't you try to do the first problem, and then we'll figure out where you're getting lost."

Noah glanced at her for a moment, an unreadable expression on his face. Ashlyn stared back, frozen in place by the force of his attention. He was so painfully... *hot*. Her friends would've laughed their asses off if they knew she thought so. His shoulder-length black hair was always a mess, his face covered in unshaven scruff. He had perpetual shadows beneath his heavy-lidded eyes, but no matter how sleepy or unfocused he looked, those eyes were like lasers. Ice blue and clear as crystal. She even liked his baggy, rumpled clothes. They made her think of him on his skateboard—so focused and talented and sharp.

Finally, Noah looked away from her, releasing her from whatever spell his stupid beautiful face always put her under.

"Right," he said, sounding skeptical. "Let's see where I get lost."

She watched as he worked through the problem—finding the cotangent—and waited for him to slip up. But he didn't. He did the problem just fine, with no hesitation, and came out with the correct answer.

"Um, yeah, that's right. You got that one," Ashlyn said, trying not to sound too surprised. "Go ahead and do the next one."

She watched again as he went through the problem with little effort and came out with the correct answer again.

"Okay... do the next one?" she said uncertainly.

Problem by problem, Ashlyn watched as Noah sailed through them. The only one he got wrong was because he'd accidentally mistyped one number on the graphing calculator. Once he put in the right value, he got the right answer.

"I don't understand," Ashlyn said, staring at his scratchy handwriting. "Only failing students are required to do tutoring. Did you... *ask* to be tutored?"

Noah scoffed. "No."

"Then how on earth are you failing? You obviously know what you're doing."

Noah shrugged sullenly.

There was only one thing she could think of. "Are you not turning in the homework?"

Noah didn't answer her, scowling down at his notebook.

"*Seriously*, Noah? You're failing on purpose? What the hell?"

He didn't answer her, just started packing up his notebook and textbook. He slid the calculator back to her. "Thanks, Princess."

She gritted her teeth at the old insult. It never bothered her when Tyler Kemp or Nate Vogel or any one of those scrubby losers called her "Princess," but for some reason, it really hurt when Noah did.

"Noah—"

"See you." He pushed out of his chair and slung his backpack over one shoulder, turning away from her. She watched him walk away, aggravated and sad at the same time.

Stupid to care, she told herself. Noah didn't like her. He thought she was a prissy little goody-two-shoes.

He was probably right.

four

ASHLYN RETURNED TO THE TABLE, heart hammering, hands shaking. She passed the drinks around and slid back into the booth beside Rose. Laila and Dia were seated on the other side of the booth, thanking her with smiles as they accepted their drinks.

Laila, tall and slender, looked like a super model with her waist-long box braids, high cheekbones, and rich, dark skin. Next to her, Dia looked like a Hollywood golden age bombshell, short and buxom, with enormous dark eyes and gleaming black hair styled in shoulder-length waves. Beside Ashlyn, Rose was all vibrant color and cool Slavic beauty. Of the four of them, Ashlyn was definitely the plain one, and while she didn't usually dwell on that sort of thing too much, she was excruciatingly aware of it right now.

Why didn't anybody warn her that Noah Sorenson had become hot as hell since she'd left town? *God.* In high school, despite the fact that he'd hated her, she'd had a torturous crush on him. Even though he'd been the antithesis of everything she'd ever wanted for herself—no ambition, no discipline, no self-awareness. Back then, he'd looked like the sickly lovechild of Gomez Addams and Kurt Cobain. And, if she was being honest with herself, it had totally worked for her.

But now he was an intimidating, grown-ass man. His thick black hair was shorn short, his angular jaw covered in a dense but neatly-trimmed beard. His eyelashes were just like she remembered—thick and long and curling. A fairy-tale princess would've killed for those eyelashes. His eyes were still an arresting cobalt blue, but instead of watching her with lazy humor the way they used to, now they pierced her like a knife.

"Are you okay?" Rose asked.

Ashlyn blinked, plastering on a carefree smile. "Yeah, sorry, I was just thinking. I ran into Noah and Wes Sorenson at the bar."

Everyone looked over. "*Ooooh...* the Sorenson boys," Laila said, pretending to fan herself.

"Right?" Rose agreed emphatically.

Dia stared down at her beer, her dark hair swinging around the sides her face like curtains.

"What happened with Noah?" Ashlyn asked. "Back in high school, he was kind of..." she trailed off, unable to find a charitable way to describe what a magnetic, fascinating train wreck he'd been.

Laila shrugged. "One day he just seemed to get his shit together."

"My brother hung out with him a lot right after high school," Rose said. "They both worked random construction jobs and got high all the time. One day, it was like Noah just decided to... I don't know... be better? He stopped doing drugs, stopped drinking, enrolled at the tech college. And now he's *that*." Rose gestured vaguely in the direction of the iron-jawed, flinty-eyed, muscle man who basically saved Ashlyn from falling flat on her face and then stared daggers at her while she tried to make small talk.

Ashlyn cast a discreet look in his direction. He and his brother were engrossed in an intense conversation, totally oblivious to her. She watched as they talked, unable to stop herself.

Noah had been her first kiss. She didn't think even he knew that. They'd been seventeen, all her friends had already started dating, and a bunch of them had already gone as far as having sex. Meanwhile, Ashlyn hadn't so much as kissed anyone else—and she hadn't expected to. Not until after she graduated and moved away. She had no intentions of falling for a local and getting locked into Lenora forever.

But, for two people who had absolutely nothing in common, Noah and Ashlyn were always running into each other. When she was leaving soccer practice, he was always by the bleachers with his burnout friends. When she was showing up to pick up her drunk friends from yet another ill-advised underage drinking party, he was there to mock her for being an uptight priss. When she was volunteering because she needed an excuse to avoid home and pad out her college applications, he was there working off one court-ordered sentence or another.

Noah had never strung her along or given her the impression he saw her as anything other than a boring goody-two-shoes. But she'd liked his irreverent sense of humor and she'd convinced herself that his constant mocking hid a secret affection. Towards the end of their senior year, she'd thrown all caution to the wind and he'd shut her down—hard. To this day, she still didn't know what she'd done wrong. It had made her paranoid. It had taken nearly two years before she found the nerve to kiss another guy because she'd been terrified that she was awful at it, and would just face more of the same callous rejection.

"Hey, uh, Ashlyn? Are you trying to use telepathy on him, or something?" Laila asked.

Ashlyn jerked her gaze away from Noah, mortified. "Sorry, what?" She laughed nervously. "No. Uh... no."

The three of them regarded her suspiciously.

If she didn't say something, they were going to jump to absurd conclusions. "I was just... Noah didn't like me in high school. And apparently that hasn't changed." She shrugged. "I shouldn't let it bother me."

Rose's brows drew together. "What do you mean? What did he say?"

"Nothing. It's fine. He was just, you know, a little cold." She racked her brain for a way to shift the conversation.

She was saved when Dia abruptly straightened, staring at the door with wide-eyed alarm. The rest of them turned to see what made her react.

Two more Sorensons walked in—just as raven-haired and gorgeous as all the others. It was Lucas and the only Sorenson sister, his fraternal twin, Rowan. They were three years younger than Ashlyn, and she hadn't known the younger Sorensons as well as she'd known the elder three.

The latest arrivals crossed the bar to where their brothers sat. Dia's gaze tracked them the whole way.

"You still with us, Dee?" Laila asked, nudging her.

Dia spun back to face her friends, flushing deep red. "What?"

Laila and Rose exchanged bemused smiles. Rose reached over, nudging Dia's beer closer to her.

"Go on, fill yourself up with liquid courage and shoot your shot."

It didn't seem possible, but Dia flushed an even deeper shade of red. "No."

"Which one?" Ashlyn asked, sipping her beer as she eyed the youngest Sorenson twins.

"Nobody," Dia said heatedly.

"Lucas," Laila and Rose said at the same time.

Dia shot them a betrayed look. "I can't. I seriously just *can't*. He's my neighbor *and* we work together. If he shot me down, I would have to quit my job and move to a new state."

"That seems like an overreaction," Rose said mildly, hiding a smile.

The conversation moved onto other things. The other three filled Ashlyn in on all the biggest changes since she'd left town—who got married, who got divorced, who had kids, who burnt down their furniture store and ended up going to prison for insurance fraud and arson... the usual small town catch-up. As the night went on, a few more familiar faces from high school came over to say hi. Conversations ebbed and flowed. The bar began to thin out. Before Ashlyn knew it, she was yawning into her fifth beer and trying to remember why she'd wanted to leave Lenora so badly.

As the four of them stepped out into the night, she lifted her face to the sky and took a deep breath. Even in the middle of town, the surrounding pine-covered ridges made the air clean and fresh. The sky was clear, revealing a nearly-full moon and a tapestry of twinkling stars. At the edge of town, Lake Lenora was as still as glass, reflecting dark and beautiful against the sky.

It was such a far cry from the last few years of her life that she had to pause on the sidewalk, drinking it in. The buildings were low and cosy, leaving the whole sky open above her. The stars were brighter and sharper than she'd seen them in a long time.

After she found out that she was Grandma's sole heir, she'd spent days dreading her return here. But why? The woman who'd made it so miserable for her was gone. Ashlyn had feared her for so long that she'd let her memory overshadow all the good things in Lenora. She'd forgotten the beauty of the land, the familiar comfort of the people she'd grown up with. She'd forgotten how nice it was to live here when her grandma wasn't breathing down her neck.

"Alright, not to name names, *Ashlyn*," Rose said with a drowsy smile, "but somebody convinced me to have a few more rounds than I normally would. So who knows somebody who can drive me home?"

Dia and Laila leaned against each other, arms linked. "I need a ride, too," Laila said.

"Me three," agreed Dia.

"Get an Uber," Ashlyn said, pulling out her phone.

In unison, the other three burst into laughter.

"Where do you think we are?" Laila demanded, still laughing as she gestured up and down the quiet main street. "There are no Ubers here."

Ashlyn flushed, mildly embarrassed. She'd been in Chicago too long. "Whoops. Well, maybe——"

Behind them, Wes and Noah Sorenson stepped out of the bar.

"Noah!" Rose crowed, pointing at him.

Noah froze, eyebrows shooting up.

"You up to driving a few drunks home?" Rose asked with what she must have considered a winning smile.

Noah returned her lopsided grin with a wry one of his own. "Guess I can't say no." His gaze met Ashlyn's. "Looks like the tables have turned, hey, Ash?"

Ash. Nobody outside of Lenora ever called her that. And the last time she'd heard Noah call her that, she'd been a pining, heartsick teenager who still didn't know what she'd done wrong with that failed kiss.

"Maybe for you," she said, sounding colder than she'd meant to. She stepped back from them all. "I can walk. I'm staying just up the road at the Hideaway."

Noah frowned, his gaze sliding three blocks down to the little motel. "What, you're too good to stay at your grand-ma's?" He said it lightly, but there was a bite to his words that made her spine stiffen.

Stay in that piss-soaked hoarder's nightmare? "Yes," she said flatly. "I am."

She turned her back and walked away.

"Bye, Ashlyn!" Rose called.

"Bye!" Laila and Dia chorused.

"See you 'round," Wes called.

She waved to them all over her shoulder and walked on.

No doubt about it. Noah Sorenson still hated her. And she *still* didn't know why.

five

THE NEXT MORNING, Noah got a call from his office manager just as he was pulling up to the lodge at Lake Lenora Resort.

"Hey, Noah. Can you spare anyone on the crew? We need somebody to do a walkthrough and offer a quote for structural repairs."

He paused, truck door open, one foot braced on the running board. "How bad is it?"

"I'm not sure. Residential home, three bedrooms, about fifteen hundred square feet. It sounds like several years of neglect. Could be terrible. Could be fine."

Both the guys he'd normally send for an assessment were currently overseeing different phases of the rebuild at the resort. He pulled his foot back into the truck and shut the door. "I'll handle it. Will you text me the address? Thanks, Amy."

As soon as he pulled up to the address Amy gave him, he cursed. It was Judy Vandale's house—the house Ashlyn

Vandale grew up in. Which meant his client was none other than his teenage nemesis.

He sighed heavily, giving himself a moment before he schooled his features into a neutral expression and stepped out of the truck. As he walked up the path to the front door, he was startled by movement on the porch swing. Ashlyn was sitting there, waiting for him.

"Oh. Noah." She regarded him flatly. "I wasn't expecting you."

"You called Sorenson Contracting, and you're surprised that a Sorenson showed up?"

"I was surprised that *you* showed up."

"Who were you expecting?" he asked tersely.

She shrugged. "I don't know. Wes, maybe. Or James."

Obviously, she hadn't expected Noah, the loser brother, to be a business owner. "Sorry. I'm the only Sorenson on the payroll. You want to call a different contractor?"

For a second, she looked like she might say yes. But she only shrugged and turned towards the front door. "I'm sure you'll be fine."

He bit back a caustic reply while she fished the key out of her pocket and opened the door.

The smell hit him a split second before his eyes adjusted to the dim interior. The place was an absolute wreck. Ashlyn had pulled her sweater over her mouth and nose. Noah did the same with his flannel. His eyes watered at the god-awful pungency of cat urine mingling with rotten garbage and mildew. Resisting the instinct to walk away, he followed her inside. The floor bowed beneath each footstep. The subfloor was rotten, and probably not even safe to walk on.

"What the hell happened here?" he asked, staring at the heaps of junk that overflowed the front room and lined the walls in the hallway. There were stacks of old magazines, boxes filled with unopened mail, broken and mismatched furniture stacked with all kinds of knick-knacks, from beautiful blown glass sculptures to creepy porcelain dolls to dusty old McDonald's toys. Garbage bags filled with mystery contents sagged in heaps in the corners.

"This is what happened after I moved out," Ashlyn said, voice muffled by the sweater clasped over her face.

"Did you know this was happening?"

"I suspected."

"And you never checked in on her?" he demanded, appalled. She'd just left that poor old woman to drown in her own inability to care for herself?

"Not once." Ashlyn stared back at him, eyes cold and unflinching. "So are you going to tell me what needs to be done to fix this place, or what?"

He didn't understand how Lenora's prodigal sweetheart could have so callously abandoned the woman who raised her, but he let it drop. Judy was gone and there wasn't anything that could be done for her now. "It'd be easier if this place was cleared out. But the flooring's definitely going to need to be ripped up and replaced. I'd be worried about mold in the walls, too. I can't give you a solid quote when so much of the structure is hidden beneath all this junk."

Her shoulders slumped. "You know anybody I can pay to do the cleanup?"

"Come out to the truck with me. I can give you Jeanne Campbell's card. She mostly does commercial structures, but she takes big residential projects, too." A part of him wanted to judge her for not rolling up her sleeves and doing the work herself, but he couldn't. It was an enormous job— the kind that called for respirators, strong backs, and a big dumpster.

Ashlyn stood beside the truck as he dug out one of Jeanne's cards. As he turned to hand it to her, he was hit by a memory so powerful, for a split-second he lost sense of time. He was seventeen years old, looking at her just like this —him in the seat of his car, her standing beside the open door, avoiding eye contact. They'd both been leaving their volunteer shift at the food pantry, and her grandma hadn't come to pick her up, so Noah had given her a ride. She'd seemed so nervous and it had sparked the completely ridiculous notion in his head that she might like him—*like* him, like him.

He'd been wrong. God he'd fucked that up so badly.

He snapped back to the present and felt his face heat at the memory. It made him want to crush the business card in his fist. He was a grown man. He'd survived depression and addiction and had come out the other side stronger and healthier. He owned a successful business and was good at what he did. He'd enjoyed the company of beautiful women before. And yet, here he was, blushing like a nervous virgin at his first co-ed dance.

"Is that her card?" Ashlyn prompted.

He passed it to her awkwardly, mashing it into her hand. "Fuck. Sorry. Let me get you a new one."

She smoothed it between her fingers. "It's fine. I can read it." She slid it into her coat pocket. "Thanks."

"No problem. Give me a call when the place is cleaned out, and I can come by to take another look at it."

"What do I owe you for today?"

He waved her off. "Don't worry about it."

"Alright. Well. Thanks." She stepped back from the truck, giving him room to pull the door shut. Her gaze lifted to the house and her guarded expression turned bleak.

"I know you want to get the hell out of here, but

Jeanne's fast. Her crew will get this place emptied out in a day or two, and then I can get back in here."

She nodded, her troubled gaze still tracing over the house. "Good," she said softly. "I just want it done."

He couldn't help but stare at her. He knew she was a cold-hearted ice princess. But in this moment, she just looked so lost. His instinct was to pull her into his arms. It aggravated him that he was still so susceptible to her. He'd grown and matured in countless ways—but apparently he was still a self-destructive tool when it came to Ashlyn Vandale.

Noah's mouth worked without his brain's permission. "Do you hate it here that much?"

Her gaze dropped back to him. There's something unreadable in those fathomless brown depths. "I don't hate it here. I never hated it here."

He frowned. "Then why—"

She fell back a step. "Thanks for coming by," she said abruptly. "Sorry to have wasted your time. I'll call when the place is cleared out. Bye."

She turned and walked away. He pulled his door shut and watched in his side mirror until she got into her own vehicle and drove away.

before

OF COURSE ASHLYN VANDALE was here. Of
course she was. When Noah was sentenced to community
service to work off too many underage drinking citations,
he'd decided to volunteer at the food pantry on the far side
of town, since most of the other community service losers
tended to sign up for park maintenance. That way he
wouldn't have to deal with any of them. Tyler and Nate
were fine, but Kyle, Dan, and Allie were hard to put up with
for long.

But Noah would've gladly spent his community service
hours dealing with their idiocy if it meant he didn't have to
face the angelic Ashlyn Vandale. There was no way she was
here to serve a community service sentence. Saint Ashlyn
was definitely volunteering purely out of the goodness of
her sweet little heart.

The orientation for volunteers took place in a small
conference room, which had probably originally been a
closet of some kind that they'd managed to fit a table
inside. It was a circular table, with the volunteer coordi-

nator already sitting at twelve o'clock, Ashlyn positioned at three o'clock, and several other chairs already taken by other people. So, Noah had two options—sit on the other side of the table from Ashlyn, where she'd be as far away as possible, but looking directly at him. *Or* sit closer to her, so she wouldn't be able to look at him without turning to face him.

He told himself he was just sparing himself her judgmental looks when he took the seat next to her. He was technically "behind" her since she was sitting with her body angled toward the coordinator. She'd have to turn around to say anything to him.

Which she did.

"Hey, Noah. I didn't know you volunteered."

Instead of being annoyed that she'd spoken to him, he was happy. And his happiness annoyed him. "It's not really 'volunteering' when it's court-ordered, is it?" he said flatly.

Her eyes widened briefly. "Oh." She clearly didn't know what to say to that.

Taking pity—another annoying impulse—he added, "But I chose the food pantry since I figured it's a good cause."

Ashlyn's expression softened and it made his stomach flip. He looked away from her, pretending to be interested in the paperwork laid out in front of his seat.

A few seconds later, the coordinator stood up and started speaking, and Noah was spared having to make any more conversation.

At the end of the night, he hadn't really done any "volunteering," but the orientation still counted towards his community service, so he had to wait until all the good people had filed out of the room so he could ask the volunteer coordinator to sign off on his service log.

"Two hours down," she told him with a twinkling smile, seemingly unbothered by the fact that he was here on a judge's orders. "How many more to go?"

"Thirty-eight."

"Aw, that won't take long at all. I had to do two hundred hours when I was your age for stealing a car."

Noah did a double take at the smiling, apple-cheeked, middle-aged lady. "You what?"

She shrugged. "It was good for me. It got me interested in community organizing and mutual aid networks, and here I am now." She gestured around the grim-looking conference room, her contentment undaunted.

"Right. Well, thanks." Noah waved his log sheet in acknowledgment before folding it up and tucking it in his pocket. "See you later."

As he stepped out of the building into the fading light of evening, he saw Ashlyn walking out of the parking lot, onto the graveled shoulder of the road.

"Ashlyn!" he called.

She jumped, startled, and spun back to face him.

"What are you doing?" He trotted to catch up with her.

"Going home," she answered.

He stared at her incredulously. "You're going to *walk* home?"

"It's only a couple miles," she said defensively.

"Yeah, and most of it's along a county highway!" He gestured emphatically at the road. It was a curvy, narrow stretch of two-lane highway that wound its way through dense forest before coming back into town.

"Well, my grandma needed the car to get to choir practice, so I don't really have a choice."

"Yes you do, you lunatic. Come on, I'm driving you home."

Ashlyn stuttered to a halt. "What? No. I can't—you live outside of town, and I live—"

"Oh *no*," Noah said sarcastically, "It'll take me an extra five minutes to swing by your house. However will I make up the lost time?"

Ashlyn regarded him tensely, silently.

"Come on, Ash. If you walk home, I'm just going to idle alongside you the whole way."

She smiled, and then the smile turned into a small bubble of laughter that made his stomach do another stupid flip.

"Alright. Fine," she huffed. Maybe realizing that she sounded a bit ungrateful, she added more gently, "Thank you."

"Come on," Noah said, turning back to the parking lot, avoiding any kind of sincerity or sentiment. "The extra five minutes already turned into six."

His car was a rusty old Honda Civic with a mostly red body, but a black hood and a blue driver's side door. Ashlyn didn't comment on the mismatched colors or the missing hubcaps or the duct tape holding his rearview mirror to the windshield, and the car thanked her for it by nearly garroting her with the automatic seatbelt.

"Sorry—should've warned you about that."

"It's fine," she said, face flushed as she untangled a hank of her hair from the seatbelt.

"You live over by Merrick Park, right?"

"Yeah. Right across from it."

Noah could feel her looking at him, but he kept his eyes forward as he started the car and put in it in gear. At first, the drive was awkwardly silent. Neither of them spoke as he pulled onto the highway.

After what felt like a lifetime of dead silence, Ashlyn said, "What'd you do?"

He was so hyper-attuned to every molecule of air separating the two of them that he didn't immediately grasp the question. "What?"

"What'd you do to get sentenced to community service?"

"Underage drinking citation."

"They give community service for that?" Ashlyn seemed surprised, which in turn surprised Noah. He would've expected her to have a harsher view on rule-breaking.

"They give you community service if you rack up enough of them."

"Oh." She was quiet for a second. "How many is enough?"

Noah let out a sigh. He knew what he was. He knew Ashlyn knew what he was. But spelling it out for her was excruciating. "Three strikes and you're out."

"Just three? You must get away with a lot."

Noah choked on a surprised laugh. "What's that supposed to mean?"

"I mean, every time I have to pick up my friends' drunk asses from some party, you're there, too. If you only got caught three times, that's pretty good odds."

"Your drunk little friends have never been caught."

She considered that. "Hmm. You're right. You're actually really bad at this. You need to be sneakier."

"*Ashlyn Vandale*," Noah uttered her name in scandalized tones. He was hamming it up, but it wasn't far off from his real feelings. The perfect Princess was telling him to get better at concealing illegal activity?

Ashlyn laughed and smiled at him. He had to force his attention back to the road so he didn't kill them. Ashlyn's smiles were lethal. He never saw her smile like that—so open and carefree. Definitely not at *him*. He snuck one more look at her. She was still smiling, but there was a contemplative quality to her expression.

"You know…" She trailed off. "Never mind."

"What?"

"Nothing."

"Just tell me."

"It's nothing."

"Ashlyn."

"Noah."

"*Ashlyn.*"

She muttered something under her breath.

"What?"

"I said—" the rest was lost in muttering.

"*What?*"

"You're actually a really nice person!" Ashlyn burst out, almost angrily.

Noah cracked a smile. "*That's* what you were too embarrassed to tell me? That I'm *nice?*"

"Shut up."

"You *should* be embarrassed," Noah went on. "Embarrassed that it took you so long to realize how nice I am. I'm incredibly nice. Everyone thinks so. In fact, I—"

"Oh my god, shut up."

"—think I'm nicer than *you*, Princess."

"Don't call me Princess!"

"See? I don't scream at people who give me flattering nicknames."

"It's not flattering!" she objected hotly, but the last word broke on a bubble of laughter.

"I also don't encourage criminal delinquents to get better at being criminal delinquents."

"That's not what I was—"

"And I definitely don't aid and abet other criminal delinquents by driving them home from illicit events."

"You can't when you're one of them," Ashlyn shot back with a laugh.

Something warm and glowing settled in his chest. Ashlyn Vandale was in his car, inches away from him, laughing with him. It was surreal.

All too soon, they reached her house. He pulled up to the curb and put the car in park. Surprising him yet again, Ashlyn didn't immediately lunge out of the vehicle. Instead, she turned to face him.

"Thank you for the ride," she said softly, sincerely. "I meant it before. You're really nice."

The temptation to turn it into a joke again was there, but Noah ignored it. "Any time, Ash."

Silence fell between them, but it didn't feel awkward. Noah didn't want to break it. But movement drew his eye beyond Ashlyn, to the big front window of her grandma's house. The curtains twitched aside and Judy Vandale's face peered out.

Ashlyn followed the line of his gaze, looking over her shoulder. She stiffened.

"Oh. That's my— I have to go. Thanks, Noah. See you at school." And then she was nearly beheaded by the automatic seatbelt again when she tried to escape from the car. "Ah! Jesus, that thing!" She ducked beneath it and slipped out of the car. "Bye, Noah!" The door slammed shut behind her, and he watched as she sprinted to the front door.

Her grandma pulled the door open as soon as Ashlyn

reached it, and Ashlyn stepped inside, swinging it shut immediately.

He wasn't surprised that she didn't want her grandma to them together. Everyone knew Noah was the fuck-up Sorenson. But she'd said he was *nice*. And she'd smiled at him. And laughed with him.

And it hurt.

six

THE TASK of cleaning out Grandma's house would have taken Ashlyn weeks on her own, if not a couple of months. Jeanne's crew got it emptied out in two days. As they'd cleared out everything, they'd set aside a few things they'd assumed would be sentimental to Ashlyn—including a picture of her grandparents on their wedding day and the urn containing her grandfather's ashes. The grandfather who'd died when she was a toddler, and who she had no memory of.

She didn't want the picture or the ashes, but throwing them away felt wrong. So they were tucked out of sight in her motel room's safe.

As for the rest of the house, it'd been completely stripped. The carpets were absolutely unsalvageable, so Jeanne'd had her guys pull them up and toss them in the dumpster with just about everything else. The house didn't reek as badly as it did before, but it was still disgustingly pungent. The cat urine had soaked through the carpet and padding down to the subfloor, permeating and rotting the plywood.

Ashlyn stood behind Noah in the entryway as he looked it all over. He was wearing a toolbelt today, just a big leather pocket thing over one hip that made him look like an old West gunslinger. Coupled with a well-worn gray flannel shirt and his sturdy work boots, he was the picture of rugged, masculine competence. The sight hit her just as hard as his oversize Slipknot hoodies and baggy jeans and skater shoes used to. Except there was something more to it now, because her attraction to the competent man standing in front of her was compounded by the memory of the all-consuming crush she'd had on the teenage delinquent.

Her eye was helplessly drawn to the sight of that broken-in flannel stretching across the broad muscles of his back as he moved. Thank god his back was turned, because she suddenly felt herself flushing. She plucked at the collar of her sweater, trying to cool herself before he turned and saw her turning bright red for no reason.

Using a utility knife with the blade retracted, Noah tapped at a spot in the wall. The plaster crumbled away like dried toothpaste. For a moment, Ashlyn forgot her inconvenient attraction and stared in dismay at the hole in the wall.

"Well, that can't be good," she said grimly.

"It's not." Noah continued to nudge at the wall, making more and more plaster fall away. He slid the blade out and glanced at her. "Alright if I cut into the sheetrock?"

She shrugged. Like she had any idea what should be done. "Go ahead."

He cut a neat square and knocked it out. Pulling a flashlight from his toolbelt, he shone it into the new opening and grimaced.

"What?" she asked, dread rising.

"You've got mold. This wall is going to have to be replaced." He glanced up at the ceiling where a brownish water stain mottled the plaster. "And the joists in the ceiling here. You're going to want to have a plumber look at that—" he gestured to the water stain over their heads "—and you'll need an electrician to look over the wiring. I have two electricians on my crew, and I can give you references for a plumber."

Ashlyn nodded wordlessly. It was all becoming so much more work than she'd expected. She looked around the derelict, empty house, and felt her pulse start to race. All the time, all the work, all the years she'd spent trying to keep up with her grandma's hoarding and neglect, and it'd all been so pointless. In the end, she was still saddled with the ruins of Grandma's carelessness. The work just never ended. And she was never going to escape the suffocating control.

"Ashlyn? Are you alright?" Noah was standing right next to her, but his voice sounded far away, like she was underwater.

"Yeah," she said tightly. God, she had to get out of here. She couldn't breathe. She couldn't think.

"Ashlyn? Are you—"

"Sorry. I—" She turned away from him, going for the door on shaky legs. She stumbled down the porch and into the front yard. She kept walking until she reached her car, parked alongside the curb. The whole time, she berated herself. Stupid to let herself get so worked up. *She's gone.* She was gone and once Ashlyn got the disgusting house squared away, she'd never have to think about her grandma again. But it didn't feel like that. It felt like Grandma was still here, still breathing down her neck, and if she did this wrong, if every aspect wasn't perfect, then everything would come crashing down.

"Ashlyn?" Noah followed her out, because of course he did. That's what you do when someone acts irrationally. You make sure they're not going to walk into traffic or something.

When Ashlyn was younger, she used to hide panic attacks at school by going to the bathroom and locking herself in a stall until she could breathe again. But she hadn't had to deal with one of those in a long time. It took her a couple of minutes to figure out what was even going on. When she did, she laughed in a way that must have been fairly alarming and pressed her forehead to the cool, damp roof of her car.

She felt a big hand on her back. "Ash. Breathe."

She nodded, gulping in air like a drowning woman.

"What's going on? Is it all the work? You can just sell the house as-is. Let the buyer fix it."

She shook her head. "I can't. I have to see it done. It'll never get out of my brain if I don't."

Noah was quiet for a second. The warm pressure of his hand remained on her back, right between her shoulder blades. She wanted to arch up into his touch like a cat. It was mortifying to want someone who clearly disliked her and had been forced into the position of comforting her, but it still helped. His touch anchored her. She wasn't thinking about her grandma or the house or all the stuff that needed to be done. The only thing on her mind was the feel of Noah's hand.

"What's going on here?" Noah asked quietly. He took his hand away and crossed his arms over his chest, frowning at her. Not an angry frown. He looked confused. Worried, even. For her?

"I..." How did she explain? He thought she was an asshole for leaving town and never looking back. How could she explain that the sweet old widow who played the organ at St. Joseph's every Sunday and ran an annual charity drive for cancer research and oh-so-selflessly took in her orphaned granddaughter—how did she explain that that lady was actually kind of a monster? Nobody believed it back when she'd tried to get help from Sister Jeanne and Father Dan. And now that Judy Vandale was dead and had basically been canonized by the parish, people were even less likely to believe it.

Noah was still looking at her. He may have been all grown and muscular and cleaned-up, but those cobalt blue eyes were the same as they'd been more than a decade ago. Back when the two of them had always been at odds. Back when she'd kissed him and he'd scorned her.

"Nothing. I'm fine. Sorry." She stepped back from him. "I trust your judgment. Whatever you think needs to be done, go ahead and do it."

"Don't you want—"

"As fast as you can get it done," she said, looking down as she fished her keys out of her pocket. "I'd appreciate it." She moved quickly to the driver's side and slipped into her car. "Sorry to run, but I've got a meeting I have to be at."

He ran a hand through his thick black hair, looking irritated. "I'll have Amy e-mail you the estimate."

"Sounds good. Thanks, Noah. Bye." She shut her door and start the engine, pulling away while Noah stood on the curb, watching her go.

seven

NOAH SWUNG by the office to drop off the paperwork for Ashlyn's estimate before heading back to the resort. Amy Mueller, his office manager, looked it over, glasses pulled down on her nose. At first glance, Amy seemed fairly unassuming—a short, plump woman whose desk was covered in pictures of her children and grandchildren. But woe betide the fool who mistook amiability for weakness. He'd seen Amy make burly subcontractors stammer in shame when she'd caught them cutting corners. Even Noah didn't dare cross her.

"And how's our little Ashlyn doing?" Amy asked, sliding the papers onto her desk.

He shrugged, not comfortable sharing that Ashlyn had basically hyperventilated and had to run out of the house. "She can't wait to get this house fixed so she can get the hell out of Lenora."

Amy nodded as if that's what she expected. "Can't blame the girl."

"Why? What's so bad about this town?"

"I don't think it's Lenora she wants to get away from."

"Then what is it?"

Amy pursed her lips, looking conflicted. "They say you shouldn't speak ill of the dead."

Noah raised his eyebrows impatiently. "When have you ever cared about mincing words?"

Amy shot him a half-hearted glare. "This is mostly speculation on my part. But my family went to St. Joseph's—Judy's church—and I remember Judy being somewhat of a… well, a heinous bitch."

He blinked. He couldn't have been more surprised if she'd told him Judy was secretly still alive and living on the moon with Elvis and JFK.

"Most people think Judy Vandale was one of God's own angels," Amy continued. "But anybody who had to work closely with her knows she was hell to deal with. I was in the church choir, and I quit because I couldn't handle Judy's bullying. I can't imagine she was much better at home, where social pressure wasn't forcing her to be at least marginally courteous."

Noah's stomach churned. "You think she was abusive?"

Amy shrugged. "It's just speculation. For all I know, Judy was a bitch to the rest of us, but a doting grandmother to Ashlyn."

He thought back to Ashlyn's reaction this afternoon. Her face pale, eyes unfocused, breathing ragged. All that, just from setting foot in her childhood home.

"No," he said slowly, mind spinning to reframe so much of what he'd thought he knew about Ashlyn Vandale. "No, I don't think she was."

"Poor Ashlyn," Amy said sympathetically.

God, he was an asshole.

· · ·

THE NEXT MORNING, NOAH SWUNG THROUGH RUBY'S CAFE for coffee before he had to head out to Lake Lenora Resort. He had two of his guys putting down a new subfloor at Ashlyn's grandma's house, and a plumber he trusted was coming in to take a look at the upstairs bathroom. He wasn't expecting to see Ashlyn until later, though part of him felt he should find her right away and apologize. But what would he even say? *Sorry I was silently judging your traumatic past that I'm not supposed to know about?*

So he grabbed his coffee and was almost to the door when it swung open and Ashlyn Vandale stepped inside. Her gaze met his and, for a second, they both froze.

"Oh," she said, those warm brown eyes pinning him in place. "Uh, Noah. Hi."

"Hey," he said. It came out too abrupt, like it'd been torn out of him. It sounded impatient and surly. He cleared his throat. "Uh, how are you?"

Surprise briefly flashed across her face. "I'm fine," she said, sounding a little uncertain. "How are you?"

"Good." He nodded.

She smiled.

It was painfully awkward.

"Well, I just came to get a coffee before I swing by the estate attorney's office," she said, stepping around him. "Nice seeing you."

"Wait, Ash—"

Surprise crossed her face again, and he realized he'd called her by her old nickname. Was it too familiar for him? Maybe only her friends got that privilege.

"—lyn," he tacked on, too late. "I'm sorry if I've seemed..."

"Prickish?" she suggested.

A flare of annoyance almost made him spit out something just as caustic, but before he did, he was overwhelmed by an unexpected wave of nostalgia. For the space of a heartbeat, he was seventeen again, trading barbs with the too-perfect girl he was half in love with.

"I've had a lot on my mind." That was somewhat true. He just didn't tell her that what'd been on his mind was *her*. "I'm sorry if I took it out on you."

She was quiet, brow furrowed, considering him. "You've changed," she said quietly.

He gestured at himself. "Well, yeah."

"I don't mean how you look. You…" She tilted her head, gaze going a little distant. "You're not as… vivid as you used to be."

"Vivid?"

She straightened, pressing her lips into a thin line. "Sorry, that was rude. I don't mean you're not still, you know… vivid. Whatever that means." Her face turned red.

Noah was fascinated. Had he ever seen Ashlyn Vandale blush? He wasn't even insulted about the vivid thing. Because mostly what he was hearing was, back when he was obsessed with Ashlyn, she'd thought he was… *vivid*.

"I guess I'm not," he said, fighting a smile. "I'm a stable, boring old man now."

She snorted. "I doubt that."

"What, that I'm stable? Or that I'm boring?"

She flushed an even deeper shade of red. "I'm going to be late for my meeting with my grandma's lawyer." She turned abruptly away from him and hurried over to the cafe counter.

"See you this afternoon," he said.

Ashlyn glanced back at him, brow furrowed, cheeks still red.

51

"Jeanne's crew is done with clean-up. My office manager spoke to you about doing a new walk-through—"

"Oh! Right. I remember." She nodded, turning away again. "Later, then. Bye, Noah."

He watched her go, a confusing churn of emotions battling inside him. Best let sleeping dogs lie, he told himself, and left.

before

"*NOAH!*" Ashlyn hissed, trying to look annoyed, but losing the fight against a smile. He'd mopped around her while she was stacking boxes of Rice-a-Roni on the shelves, trapping her in the corner. If she walked across the freshly mopped floor, she'd leave prints from her dusty shoes. To be fair, anyone else would've just walked over it anyway. But Ashlyn couldn't. She physically couldn't. At some point since they'd been volunteering together, he'd noticed that she'd go completely out of her way, or even take a flying leap, to avoid stepping on freshly mopped floors. And since he was frequently on mop duty, he'd started using that knowledge against her.

She couldn't tell him that the reason she wouldn't walk on a wet floor with her shoes was because if she did that at home, her grandma would ream her out in an endless tirade —not stopping until Ashlyn was in tears. Once she broke down, then, and only then, would grandma lay off the screaming and decide on a punishment. Messing up the floors usually meant she'd spend the next few weeks cleaning them on her hands and knees with a kitchen sponge.

Noah didn't know that. She didn't hold it against him. She knew he thought it was just a funny quirk of hers. She was glad he saw it that way. So when he did silly things like mop her into a corner, she wasn't mad, even though crushing anxiety wouldn't allow her to walk on it. She was mostly just pleased that he was paying that much attention to her.

Taking a deep breath, she eyed the distance to the next patch of dry floor. Could she jump that far?

Noah leaned on the mop, watching her do the calculations. "You'd have to be an Olympian," he told her with a smirk.

"I'm captain of the varsity soccer team," she replied smugly. She had no choice now—she had to jump. She put all her strength into it, making the leap, stretching her front leg out as far as it would go—

And landed on wet floor. She shrieked as her feet went out from under her. But she never hit the ground. Suddenly, Noah was there, arms wrapped around her waist, hauling her upright.

"Well, damn, you almost made it, Princess."

"Don't call me Princess," she huffed, turning bright red as she twisted out of his hold. She couldn't let him see how much his embrace had flustered her—how badly she wanted to plaster herself all over him.

"Come on, it's an endearment." He smiled lazily, completely unfazed by how much of her had been pressed against him just a second ago.

"Not from you, it's not."

He shrugged and turned his attention to the dusty streaks she'd made on the wet floor, mopping them away.

"Noah! Ashlyn!" Mariah Frye, the volunteer coordinator, spotted them as she stepped out of the pantry's administrative office. "How's everything going?"

"Good," Ashlyn answered immediately, feeling an irrational spike of fear that Mariah was going to yell at her for messing up the floor Noah had just mopped.

"Glad to hear it." She turned her attention to Noah. "And glad you decided to stay on with us, Noah. That says a lot about you." She gave them both one more twinkling smile before continuing on her way toward the bathrooms.

"What did that mean?" Ashlyn asked Noah.

He shrugged.

"What does she mean by 'staying on'? Were you going to finish your community service by volunteering somewhere else?" A sudden horrible thought struck her—the mopping prank wasn't playful. He was doing it because he didn't like her. He wanted to leave the food pantry because he was tired of seeing her all the time.

"No. I finished my community service last week." He stared intently at the floor as he mopped the same perfectly clean tiles over and over again. "I signed up to stay on as a regular volunteer."

"Oh." She stared at him.

He continued to mop robotically, not looking at her.

"Well. That's good," she managed to say. "I guess I was right about you being nice."

Noah finally looked up at her, a slight smile pulling one corner of his mouth. "I thought we agreed that you were really late on figuring that one out?"

"I don't remember agreeing to that."

"I do. Your exact words were, 'How could I ever have misjudged you so badly, Noah? You are too good for this world. All the angels and saints weep with envy at your goodness.'"

"Yes, that sounds exactly like me," Ashlyn said dryly, though inside she was giddy.

He wanted to stay! Which meant, at the very least, he didn't mind seeing her every Tuesday and Thursday after school. But Ashlyn thought *maybe* it might be more than that. *Maybe* he liked seeing her as much as she liked seeing him. Her stomach flipped nervously and suddenly, she couldn't look him in the eye.

"Um... I have to get some labels." She scurried off towards the supply closet.

As she ducked into the narrow hallway that led to the bathrooms and the supply closet, she heard Noah's footsteps following behind her. Those skater boy sneakers made a distinctive *shuff* sound as he walked.

"What do you need labels for?" he asked, sounding amused.

"For labeling things," she answered briskly, cheeks hot, skin prickly. She pulled open the storage door and ducked into the closet.

For a moment, she was alone in the cool dark. Then the door swung open and Noah stepped in behind her. The door thunked shut, and then it was just the two of them, standing in the dim confines of the closet.

"You running away from me, Ash?" he asked, a smile in his voice.

From the light leaking under the bottom of the door, Ashlyn could just make out his silhouette—baggy hoodie, baggy jeans, long hair tied back at the nape of his neck.

"Um..." She could hear her breath rasping in the small space. She could hear his breathing, too.

Noah stepped closer. She brutally suppressed the urge to

throw herself at him, forcing herself instead to back away. One step, and then her back hit the shelves.

Noah kept coming. He gripped the shelves on either side of her shoulders, leaning over her. "Ash..." His voice was soft, his face so close.

She couldn't help herself—she lifted up onto her tiptoes, and pressed her lips to his.

The feeling was electric and terrifying, but she couldn't pull back. It was her first kiss. She was seventeen years old, and she'd never so much as held hands with a boy before, and she was in over her head. She didn't know what to do with herself. Her hands wanted to grab him, but the rest of her was too frozen with shock at her own audacity.

After a few seconds that felt like several years, Noah pulled back. Neither of them spoke. The silence in the closet was deafening. Ashlyn stood frozen like a statue.

Finally, Noah let out a small breath of laughter. "I don't know what I expected from the perfect Princess," he said, a mocking edge to his voice.

He left the closet. Ashlyn stayed for long minutes, mortified, willing the earth to open up and swallow her. It didn't happen, of course. When she finally found the nerve to go back out and face Noah—to apologize for assaulting him— he was gone.

eight

"THANK YOU, MR. DEWITT," Ashlyn said as she rose from her chair in front of the lawyer's desk. She held out her hand to shake. "I appreciate your help."

Mark Dewitt was a gray-haired man in his late fifties and when he stood up, he towered over Ashlyn. He eyed her outstretched hand, pausing just long enough before he shook it to make his feelings clear. Mark hadn't been particularly close to her grandmother as far as Ashlyn knew, but like most people in this tiny town, he apparently believed wholeheartedly in Judy Vandale's saintly facade. And Ashlyn's disloyalty hadn't gone unnoticed.

"Thank your grandmother, not me," he said sternly. "She didn't have to leave you anything."

I wish she hadn't. Ashlyn managed to keep the words inside, offering a bland, professional smile instead as she withdrew her hand. "That's very true. I'll leave you to the rest of your work, then. Goodbye, Mr. Dewitt."

She blew out a beleaguered sigh as she pushed out the

door of Dewitt & Larsen. Her breath fogged in the cold air, drifting hazily away. Luckily she'd had the sense to bring her heaviest winter coat. She'd been away from Lenora for a long time, and she'd forgotten how cold it got. November in Lenora could be as bitter as January in Chicago. There was no snow on the ground yet, but the gray sky overhead promised it soon.

She wasn't due to meet Noah for another couple of hours, and everyone else she knew was at work. The thought of returning to her quiet, empty hotel room opened a hollow pit in her stomach, so she walked in the opposite direction, meandering away from the prettily cobbled main street and the lakeshore.

Lenora was a tourism town—packed full of vacationers in the summer who came up north for the countless beautiful lakes, the pristine forests, and the miles and miles of trails. Things died down in fall and spring, but picked up in winter with people who came for snowmobiling and ice fishing, and of course, the Lake Lenora Winter Market. But just now, in early November, when the air was cold and the trees were bare, but the lake hadn't yet frozen over and the snow wasn't quite sticking, only the locals were here.

Except Ashlyn. She was from this place, but she didn't belong here. Not anymore. Too much time had gone by. Too much had changed. The town had changed.

As she meandered down familiar streets, she was struck by the disparity. The little strip of woods that used to run along Monroe Street was gone, mowed down, and replaced by a small office suite—a dentist, a real estate agent, a UPS store, and a veterinary clinic. A few blocks over, Kuepper's convenience store, the little mom-and-pop shop where Ashlyn used to buy snacks after school, had been bought out by a big chain store. The old video rental store was now a used sporting goods store. Wayne's Diner was now a pizza place. The building that had been a video arcade when she was really young, then a laundromat, then a nondenominational church, was now a thrift shop. What had once been a tiny, two-screen cinema in a shingle-sided building had been expanded to six screens, with a fancy new brick exterior. Road construction had done away with the alley behind the post office where all the skater kids used to congregate. The houses where her friends used to live had names she didn't recognize on the mailboxes.

Not everything had changed, though. Red Arrow Park looked exactly the same, including the metal playground equipment that had been outdated even when Ashlyn was a child. The Frosty Tip, a little walk-up ice cream stand, was still in its place of pride, directly across the street from the public beach where the same old L-shaped wooden dock stretched out into the water. The Delacroix House—the historic mansion built by Lenora's founding family—still stood atop Bear Ridge, looming down over the lake and the rest of the town in all of its Gothic Revival glory. The police, fire, and EMT departments all shared the same small building. The Muellers still went all-out with their Christmas decorations immediately after Halloween.

As she rounded the corner onto Church Hill Road, she paused. Saint Joseph's Catholic Church had gotten a new roof since she'd been gone, but otherwise, it looked exactly the same. The cream brick edifice hadn't really changed since it was built in the mid-eighteen-hundreds, so she wasn't sure why she was surprised. She supposed, with her grandma gone, Saint Joseph's seemed somehow immaterial. She stood on the sidewalk, craning her neck to look up at the vaulted nave, where a small stained glass rose window shone dark against the cloud-obscured sky. It felt like she was making eye contact with a ghost.

Shaking off the unsettling feeling, she moved past the church, walking uphill to Buchanan Street, passing the house where her friend Quinn used to live. A few more blocks, a few more turns, and she found herself standing at the corner of the fields where she used to play soccer after school. The high school looked exactly as it had the last time Ashlyn had walked through its doors—two stories, red brick, metal roof. The outside looked straight out of the eighteen-hundreds, but the inside had been modernized a few years before Ashlyn had attended.

The student parking lot was full of beater cars. A few kids mingled by the entry doors, even though class was clearly in session. She squinted, then a split-second later, realized she was looking for Noah amongst them.

"What are you, a time-traveler?" she muttered to herself, turning away from the school.

She checked the time on her phone as she made her way back to Main Street. She'd been wandering for nearly two hours. She wasn't ready to go back to her hotel room, so she returned to the coffee shop and tried not to dwell on the fact that she was going to see Noah again in a few hours.

"Ashlyn!" Ruby Turner was the spitting image of her daughter Laila, only twenty-some years into the future. Her bountiful, curling hair was contained by a silk handkerchief tied with a neat bow at the nape of her neck. She had owned Ruby's Cafe for almost twenty years now. She mostly kept to the kitchen, where she baked all the gorgeous pastries on offer, but occasionally, she could be found at the counter, filling in for one of the baristas. Today was one of those days.

"Hey, Mrs. Turner," Ashlyn greeted her happily. The

Turners' house had been one of her escapes when she was a kid. Grandma had approved of the family since they were members of the same parish, so she didn't restrict Ashlyn's time at their house. And, while she'd never said anything, Ashlyn had always sensed that Ruby Turner was one of the few people who saw through her grandmother's facade.

"Laila told me you were in town. Why didn't you stop by sooner?"

Ashlyn flushed. "I was here this morning, but I didn't want to bother——"

"Don't you say it," Ruby cut her off sternly. "You better come by to say hello to me when you're in town."

"Sorry," Ashlyn said, smiling. "Won't make the mistake again."

"What are you drinking today, hon?"

"A hazelnut and vanilla latte, please."

While Ruby made her drink, she chatted with Ashlyn about what she'd been up to and how things were going.

"An accountant?" Ruby repeated, raising her eyebrows in interest. "A CPA, hm?"

"Yes…" Ashlyn said, waiting for whatever Ruby was leading up to.

"You know John Richards retired two years ago."

"Actually, no, I didn't know that." John Richards had owned a small accounting firm in Lenora. Everyone went to him for their taxes.

"Well, he did. We all had to find a new tax guy, you know? I've been using this guy all the way down in Wausau, but it'd be nice if there was somebody local to go to."

"I'm actually pretty settled in Chicago. I was made a junior partner at my firm last year."

Ruby shrugged. "Just a thought. How long are you here

for, though? Even though he's retired, John's been handling the financials for the Winter Market, but he's been making noise about wanting to step back from that. Carol—you remember Carol Travers? She runs the Winter Market's planning committee—she's been looking for a replacement for John, talking about hiring out to an accounting firm somewhere, but the rest of the committee's against it. The Winter Market is *for* Lenora, *by* Lenora, you know? They want a local."

Ashlyn nodded hesitantly.

"Anyways, if you're here over the holidays, you could take over from John and let the poor old man enjoy his retirement."

Ashlyn grimaced apologetically. "I'm not here over the holidays, though. I just came up for a day or two to settle some stuff with my grandma's estate, and then I'm heading back to Chicago."

"Oh." Ruby's face fell. "So soon. Well…" She puffed out a sigh. "It was nice seeing you after so long."

Ashlyn noted Ruby's distinct lack of condolences for her grandma's passing, which only further solidified her suspicion that Ruby knew what a nightmare Judy Vandale was. "It was nice seeing you, too. I've really missed everyone up here. I missed the town."

Ruby nodded. "When Mike wanted to move us up here from Milwaukee thirty years ago, I thought he was absolutely out of his mind. But Lenora grows on you. I don't think I could live anywhere else."

Ashlyn started to agree with her, then realized how insincere that would sound when she'd just announced her attention to return to Chicago as soon as possible. "It's a good town," she settled on lamely.

"It's too bad you can't stay for the holidays," Ruby said,

sincerely disappointed. "But here's your latte. Next time you're in the area, don't be a stranger, alright?"

Ashlyn nodded, an uncomfortable pit opening in her stomach. Once she'd taken care of what she needed to, there'd be no reason for her to ever return.

nine

WHEN THE TIME came to set out for her grandma's house, Ashlyn was wired on caffeine and a sort of nervous anticipation she hadn't felt in years. She wasn't alone as she walked back to the house. School had let out, and a handful of kids trailed ahead of and behind her. She'd graduated high school almost fifteen years ago, but in her head, she was seventeen and walking home again.

Noah's truck was already parked in front of the house when she got there. She hesitated across the street, leaning against the chainlink fence that encircled Merrick Park. In the years since Ashlyn had left Lenora, a small skatepark had been built where there used to be tetherball poles. She glanced at the swarm of kids at the skatepark, and then quickly did a double-take.

Amidst all the kids, a broad-shouldered, bearded, grown-ass man was surrounded by a small audience as he did some kind of jumpy-flippy maneuver with the board. A kickflip? Ashlyn used to have the names of all those tricks memorized, even though she didn't skate. She stared in stunned silence as the kids around Noah let out a cheer.

Grinning, Noah wheeled back around on the board and stepped off of it, kicking it up to catch it with his hand. He passed it back to a teenage boy who held his other hand out for a fist bump. As Noah reciprocated, he caught sight of Ashlyn. He said something to his little crowd of worshippers and left them, headed toward Ashlyn.

She was already standing still, but if possible, she went even more still. Seeing the changes to the town was nothing like seeing *this*. The boy she'd had such an all-consuming crush on was standing right in front of her, doing the same super-hot things that boy had always done, except he was a grown man now, and unfortunately, the man was just as attractive to her as the boy used to be.

"Hey," Noah said when he reached the fence. "Sorry, am I late? I——"

"No," Ashlyn said quickly. "You're fine. I'm just early." She was incredibly proud of how normal the words coming out of her mouth sounded. But something about her disquiet was showing, because Noah's affable expression faded into the steady, scrutinizing look that had always given her butterflies when they were kids.

"Do you——"

Another truck pulled up in front of her grandma's house, parking behind Noah's.

"Oh, hey, that's Dave Garrett. He's the plumber I asked to swing by," Noah explained, abandoning whatever train of thought he'd originally been on. "We should probably head over."

He slipped through the gap in the fence and they fell into step beside each other as they crossed the street.

"You still skateboard," Ashlyn said abruptly.

Noah grimaced. "Hardly. I can still keep my balance. That's about it."

"That was more than just 'keeping your balance'."

He smiled at her, and the butterflies that had been dormant in her stomach since high school suddenly took flight. Morning apology aside, she knew he disliked her, but just like when they were kids, he made it so easy to forget that.

"I guess I can still show off a little bit," he admitted. With a note of smugness in his voice, he added, "With steel-toed boots on, too."

Ashlyn bit her lip hard to keep a goofy smile from over-taking her face. Cocky Noah had always made her giddy. Weird that she hadn't managed to outgrow that.

"Hey, Dave," Noah said as they reached the plumber's truck.

"Noah," the other man greeted him with a hearty hand-shake. Dave Garrett was a tall, freckled man with a shaved head and a tidy gray beard. He was dressed for work in sturdy jeans and steel-toed boots, much like Noah. "And this must be Ashlyn Vandale," he said, holding his hand out to her.

She shook it. "Nice to meet you."

"I was sorry to hear about your grandma. I didn't know Judy very well, but I only ever heard good things about her."

Ashlyn felt Noah's gaze on her. She accepted Dave's condolences with a perfunctory nod, ignoring the hot, sick feeling in her chest, then quickly changed the subject by gesturing to the house. "Let me show you inside."

· · ·

AFTER DAVE HAD TAKEN A LOOK AT THE PIPES, HE ASSURED her that it would be a relatively easy job—a few lengths of pipe had to be replaced and the joins resealed, but the overall plumbing system seemed to be in alright condition. Ashlyn had expected worse news than that, but apparently most of the damage was structural stuff that Noah's crew would have to take care of.

"But I'll have to make some cuts in the floor to get at the pipes," Dave said.

"We're ripping up the bathroom subfloor anyway," Noah told him. "So have at 'em."

After a few minutes of obligatory midwestern small talk, Dave excused himself, leaving Ashlyn and Noah alone. The silence that followed Dave's departure seemed to echo around the house. His presence had been a buffer to the discomfiture of Noah. Without Dave, Ashlyn was forced to make eye contact and talk directly to Noah again.

"So... ah, you want to do your walk-through now?" Ashlyn asked uncertainly.

Noah seemed to start, as if he just remembered he'd left the stove on. "Yeah," he said abruptly. "Of course. I've seen what I need to in the bathroom. Let's look at the other rooms."

Ashlyn followed behind Noah as he went methodically through the house, taking measurements, tapping at drywall, muttering dubiously to himself, writing things down. Her presence was starting to feel superfluous when Noah turned around suddenly and crashed into her—really driving home the point that he'd forgotten her existence entirely.

"Shit, Ash!" He dropped his clipboard as he grabbed her arm, preventing her from falling on her ass. "I'm sorry. I got a little too focused on the house."

She remembered that about him—the way he'd lose himself in things, seeming oblivious to the world. He'd done it with skateboarding, of course. But, surprisingly, drawing too. She'd once walked up on him while he was sketching an elaborate forest scene on the inside cover of his trigonometry textbook, and he'd carried on drawing while she watched over his shoulder, completely unaware of her presence. He'd nearly jumped out of his skin when she'd finally said his name.

"I should've been paying attention to where you were," he said, running his hand agitatedly through his hair.

"That's okay," she told him, stepping back as he released her arm. "I probably shouldn't have been walking right behind you. I forgot how focused you can get."

He bent to retrieve his clipboard and pencil. "You remember that?" he asked.

"Yeah," she said lightly, trying to make it seem like no big deal. "It wasn't *that* long ago."

"Fifteen years," Noah said thoughtfully.

Ashlyn swallowed a sigh. Those fifteen years felt like they'd been stolen from her, even though she was the one who'd chosen to leave. "Yeah. I guess that's a while. It doesn't feel like it."

Noah let out a quiet, rueful breath. "No. It doesn't."

It was quiet for a moment. Ashlyn knew Noah was looking at her, but she couldn't bring herself to meet his gaze. Instead, she looked around the empty house from where they stood in the hallway. It didn't look anything like she remembered—no furniture, no clutter, no carpets. It was just a shell. And the relief of seeing it that way was immense. She didn't feel her grandma breathing down her neck anymore.

"What kept you away for so long?" Noah asked, startling

Ashlyn out of her own thoughts.

"My grandma," she admitted, too caught off guard to lie.

Noah didn't respond, and she knew he had to be staring at her with total incredulity. She kept her gaze trained out the bay windows in the living room, staring at an empty street.

"We didn't have a great relationship," Ashlyn explained, not sure why she was giving away so much, but at the same time, desperate for him to understand. "I know everyone thinks she was just the sweetest old lady, but——"

"No," Noah cut in. "Not everyone. I've heard she wasn't exactly a saint."

Ashlyn looked at him in surprise. "Really?"

"Since you've been back in town, I've heard that Judy was kind of… tough to deal with, sometimes."

Ashlyn puffed out a bitter laugh. "Sometimes."

"She's why you stayed away?"

Ashlyn shrugged, feeling bleak. "Yes and no. I mean, I left town for college, and then my career took me to Chicago. But I didn't bother coming back to visit, because I didn't want to see her."

"I'm sorry," Noah said quietly.

Ashlyn glanced up at him, brow furrowed. "You sound like you're apologizing."

"I am, a little. For a long time, I thought…" he trailed off, shaking his head. "It doesn't matter."

She knew what he thought—that Judy Vandale had been a sweet old lady done wrong by her ungrateful brat of a granddaughter.

"Does everyone think that?" she asked suddenly, feeling

her chest constrict. Did everybody who'd greeted her so cheerfully at the Wooden Nickel secretly think she was a callous bitch?

Noah didn't bother asking her what she meant. "I don't think so. People are curious about why you stayed away, but as far as I know, nobody thinks badly of you."

"*You* did."

He didn't deny it. "You always hated me, Ash. I was a little biased."

Her eyes went wide. "I—what? I never hated you!"

"It was pretty obvious that you did. Don't worry about it. We were kids."

"I never hated you. *You* hated me."

He smiled wryly at her. "I didn't hate you. But you definitely thought I was a burnout loser."

"Noah," she enunciated his name crisply. "I didn't hate you. I had a massive crush on you for most of high school."

Noah blinked. "You what?"

Ashlyn's face burned. *Why* had she said that? Trying to maintain some dignity, she repeated herself with the air of a woman who's Totally Over It Now. "I. Had. A. Cr—"

"No. There's no way."

"How is there *no way?*" Ashlyn was affronted for reasons she couldn't really explain.

"Because I—" Noah hesitated, red flagging his cheeks above his beard.

"What?" she prompted, fascinated.

"Because—" He scrubbed at his jaw, beard rasping under work-rough fingers. "Because I kissed you, and you were disgusted."

The affronted feeling morphed into full-blown outrage. "*You* kissed *me?* Noah Sorenson, there is one person here who kissed the other, and that person is *me*. I am the kisser. You were the disgusted kissee."

His brows shot up. "I think I'd remember if you kissed me, and I definitely wouldn't have been disgusted."

"I think *I'd* remember if *you* kissed *me*, and you were definitely disgusted."

"No, *I* kissed you. *You* were the one who shut me down."

"That's not how it happened. I have a very clear memory of making the first move——"

"Well so do I!"

They stared at each other in frustrated silence for a moment.

Noah's brows drew together. "You're talking about that day in the supply closet at the food pantry?"

Ashlyn nodded impatiently. How could he remember it any other way than Ashlyn making a move and getting shut down hard?

"But I cornered you," he said doubtfully.

"Yeah, and I kissed you when you got close enough. And then you said 'I don't know what I expected from the perfect Princess,' and walked away."

Noah looked suddenly gutted. "Ash, I'd swear on anything that *I* kissed you. And that you didn't like it. So I tried to save face by playing it off like it didn't matter."

"I didn't *not* like it. I just didn't know what to do or what to say and I was waiting for your reaction."

Noah groaned, pressing his hand against his face. "Have you spent the last however-many years thinking I'm that much of a prick?"

Ashlyn scoffed. Her face was still burning-hot, and she needed to restore her dignity somehow. "Don't flatter yourself. I haven't been pining over you since high school. I've had more important things to think about."

Noah's hand dropped, appalled expression shifting into a wry smile. "Well, now, *you* are the one who brought up the endless pining, not me."

So much for restoring her dignity.

"I didn't say endless," Ashlyn objected heatedly. "And there was no pining!"

"You sound a little defensive there, Ash."

That smirky tilt to one corner of his mouth and the gleam of the devil in those impossibly blue eyes was so familiar, so aggravating, and so attractive all at once, it left her speechless. After a moment, she managed to gather her wits, all under the saturnine gaze of Noah Sorenson—who wasn't so different from the boy she'd once known, after all. She wanted to turn the tables on him, and she didn't let herself examine the impulse too closely.

"Do I?" she asked, putting a little breathlessness into her voice as she stepped closer to him.

Noah's smirk faltered.

The two of them were standing too close, gazes locked. If Noah bent down, or Ashlyn went up on her tip-toes, they could—

A hearty knock sounded at the door, making them both flinch. Ashlyn hastily stepped back, while Noah ran his hand through his hair in another agitated pass.

"Hello?" a familiar voice called as the door eased open a crack. "It's Dave. I just came by to—oh." He spotted Ashlyn and Noah in the hallway. "Sorry for shouting. I forgot my flashlight in the upstairs bathroom. Just came back to grab it."

"Oh, yeah, of course. No problem," Ashlyn said hastily.

The two of them stood in silence as Dave went to retrieve his flashlight. When he left again, an awkward tension stretched between them.

"So…" Ashlyn began uncomfortably.

"I have a good idea of what needs to be done," Noah said, his tone totally different. He sounded like a stranger. "New flooring in all the halls, the kitchen, the upstairs bathroom, and the den, including subfloor. This wall," he laid one hand on the rotten hallway wall, "will need to be completely replaced. It's load-bearing and the timbers are rotting and covered in mold. The ceiling joists beneath the upstairs bathroom need to be replaced for the same reason. That'll be framing, sheetrock, and plaster."

"Okay."

"It's going to run you into five digits—"

"I'll recoup the cost when I sell the house." Ashlyn shrugged.

"Alright, well, I'll get this back to my office manager and she'll email you an estimate by tomorrow morning. Sound good?"

Everything felt like it was moving so fast. "I guess, yeah."

"I assume you're heading back to Chicago soon?"

Ashlyn nodded.

"Then, if we run into any issues, my office manager, Amy, will give you a call. We can send pictures of the progress for you as well."

Ashlyn looked around the gutted house. "Okay," she said, feeling anything but okay.

"Alright. Well." Noah tucked his pencil behind his ear and his clipboard beneath his left arm. He held out his free hand to shake. "If I don't see you again, then have a nice life."

The words hit her like a punch. This was it. She was leaving Lenora for good. Once the house sold, there'd be no reason at all for her to return.

She took Noah's hand and finally looked up at him. There was something brittle in his gaze, something that seemed to reflect the anxious tension in her chest.

"Uh, yeah. You, too. Have a nice life, Noah."

ten

THAT WAS IT. Her time in Lenora was over. Ashlyn left her grandma's house for the last time and felt no sense of relief, only regret. She walked back to the Hideaway and stood in her room, heart heavy, stomach leaden, willing herself to pack her things and leave. She pictured herself back in Chicago, in her quiet, empty apartment, returning to work for the soulless firm where she had only polite relationships with her coworkers, and where she spent all day helping mega-corps better maximize their outrageous profits.

She couldn't do it. She stared at her open suitcase and couldn't take a single step towards it. Without consciously making the decision, she turned around and went back outside.

The gray sky had finally delivered on its promise, and fat flakes of snow drifted lazily down. Ashlyn pulled her hood up and started walking. She followed Main Street down to the lakeshore. She'd leave first thing in the morning, she told herself. No sense making the six-hour drive to Chicago this late in the day. She'd spent one more night in Lenora, and then she'd go home.

Except when she thought of *home*, Chicago didn't come to mind.

With a sigh, she pushed away all the turbulent, confusing feelings, and set off on a walk around Lake Lenora. It was a big lake, part of a larger flowage of three other interconnected lakes. It would take an entire day to circle the entire flowage, but she could stick to just Lake Lenora if she took the old footbridge across the falls.

The edge of the lake was beginning to freeze over with delicate little crusts of ice. The migratory birds had all moved on, leaving the water quiet and open. Little ripples dotted its surface where snowflakes touched down.

Ashlyn had so many memories tied up in this place, on this water. She could see Lake Michigan from her high-rise condo, and the expansiveness of it always amazed her, but it never quite called to her in the same way the smaller inland lakes did.

As she continued walking, she moved beyond the public beach, leaving the town behind her, following the curve of the lakeshore to where it met the forest. The conifers were all still proud and green, their boughs dusted with snow. The ground beneath her feet was soft, padded with eons worth of fallen needles and carpeted with moss.

Eventually, the forest receded a bit, giving way to the private beach attached to the abandoned Lake Lenora Resort. Once upon a time, when Ashlyn was really young, the resort had been owned by two families—the Chastains and the Sorensons. The beach, though part of the resort's property, had been open to the public. Ashlyn had swum there countless times as a child. But then some kind of bad blood between the Chastains and the Sorensons ended with the Sorensons being forced out of their share of ownership. Shortly after, the Chastains ended up shuttering the resort entirely. Ashlyn wasn't sure who owned it now, but judging by the fenced-off beach, they didn't want anybody intruding on their property.

She went up to the fence anyway, looking over. The beach was different from her memories. The pavilion where people used to be able to buy drinks and snacks was gone. The small playground for little kids was gone. The swimming buoys were gone.

But the cabins that dotted the forested resort were still there, looking just like they had when Ashlyn was a kid— and probably just like they had looked when they were built in the forties. There was evidence of recent construction on the main lodge up at the top of the ridge, as well as around some of the cabins further from the lakeshore, but the whole property still had that abandoned feeling that told her it still wasn't operating. For a moment, her memories of this place —when it was alive and busy with people—overlaid the ghost in front of her. She felt briefly warm, slipping back into that sunny, happy place. But then reality intruded, and she remembered herself. She wasn't part of this place anymore. She was leaving first thing in the morning.

But no matter how many times she repeated it to herself, she couldn't shake the melancholic aversion. Thanksgiving was coming up, then Christmas, and she didn't want to spend yet another holiday season alone. In college, she went to friends' houses for Christmas break, and briefly in grad school, she'd had a boyfriend whose family took her in during Christmas. But for the past five years, she'd had nowhere to go and nobody to spend it with.

And that's what she had to look forward to this year as well. Thanksgiving would just be like any other Thursday, spent alone in her apartment, eating an ordinary supper. Her only Christmas gift would be whatever generic thing the firm gave to all the employees. Last year it had been a really nice basket of fancy cheeses and cured meats, which had ended up being Ashlyn's Christmas supper while she watched old claymation Christmas movies.

She didn't want to spend another Christmas that way.

But what was she supposed to do? Beg an invitation from people she hadn't spoken to in over a decade? She couldn't do that. She had to go back to Chicago.

Her phone buzzed in her pocket and she pulled it out. Dia had texted her.

Hope everything went okay with your grandma's house. Are you in town for much longer?

She realized she'd also missed a text from Rose: *Hey, if you're still in town, you should come to Quinn's birthday party this Friday. She'd love to see you before you leave.*

She couldn't do it, she realized abruptly. She couldn't leave. Not yet. She just needed a little more time to make her goodbyes. Instead of responding to the texts, she called her firm's Human Resources number.

"Teller and Novak Human Resources. How many I help you?"

"Hi, this is Ashlyn Vandale. I'm currently out of the office on bereavement leave, but things have gotten complicated with my grandmother's estate. I'm going to need to take an extended leave of absence."

eleven

LIKE MOST LOCALS, Noah did his grocery shopping at Larsen's rather than Girard's. Both were locally owned, and Larsen's Foods didn't have as much selection as Girard's Market, but Girard's was located close to the lake, and therefore priced for tourists. Locals ducked in there when they needed something particular, but otherwise, they saved their money.

He was in the snack aisle, frozen between two different flavors of chips. This late in the day, his meds started wearing off, and the most absurdly inconsequential decisions became more and more difficult. It didn't help that most of his brain was still stuck on Ashlyn.

Have a nice life.

He hadn't seen her in fifteen years. Now he'd never see her again.

"Oh! Noah?"

He turned to see that very same woman standing at the head of the aisle, basket over her arm, staring at him in surprise. He blinked, just to make sure his obsessing hadn't conjured a hallucination. She was still there.

"Ashlyn? I thought you left."

"Um… actually, no. Not yet. I talked to Carol Travers a couple days ago because the Winter Market's planning committee's been trying to find a replacement for John Richards, and, well… I'm the replacement."

"So you're staying?" He had to carefully modulate his voice into polite neutrality.

"Just until the New Year."

He didn't know what to say to that.

"So, anyway, just getting some groceries. Can't eat out for every meal, you know?"

He nodded wordlessly.

"Okay. Well. See you around, maybe."

She slipped past him, grabbed a bag of Cheetos, and then left the aisle. Noah did the rest of his shopping on high alert for Ashlyn sightings. He didn't see her again until they approached the only open checkout lane at the same time. Ron Larsen, the owner of the store, was a stout, cheerful man in his late sixties. He had snowy-white hair and a big beard that made him look like Santa Claus year-round. He and his wife worked the checkouts alongside their other employees, which Noah had always appreciated about him —he didn't put himself above other people.

"You look familiar," Ron told Ashlyn as she set her basket on the conveyor belt. "Do I know you?"

"Hey, Mr. Larsen. I'm Ashlyn Vandale—Judy's grand-daughter."

Ron's convivial smile dropped into a cold, closed-off expression that Noah had never seen on his face. "Ashlyn," he said flatly. "Been a while, hasn't it?" There was a wealth of judgment in that question, and Ashlyn obviously heard it.

Her shoulders stiffened slightly, her polite smile became noticeably fixed.

"Yes, it has. How have you been?"

"I've been alright," he said coolly as he scanned her groceries. "Better than some, since my grandkids still come around."

Noah felt his spine stiffen.

"Oh," Ashlyn said, obviously at a loss.

The rest of the transaction was conducted in silence until he told her the total. Ashlyn paid and then scuttled out of the store.

"Well, now, it's Noah!" Ron greeted him cheerfully—back to the man Noah recognized. "How've you been, son?"

"What was that?" Noah demanded, bristling with outrage on Ashlyn's behalf while simultaneously mortified to be calling out an elder he'd always respected.

Ron blinked. "I'm not sure I—"

"You didn't have to talk to Ashlyn like that."

"Ah." Ron's confusion subsided. "You must not know the backstory, there. Little Miss Vandale skipped town the minute—"

"I know the backstory," Noah cut him off. "I know more of it than you do, I think. Ashlyn had her reasons for leaving town. She doesn't need your judgment."

Ron was back to being confused. But he didn't argue. "I suppose I'll take your word for it, then." He cleared his throat. "How've you been otherwise, son?"

As he carried his groceries out to his truck, he spotted Ashlyn closing the trunk of her shiny black Lexus. She caught his eye, fixing him with a glowering stare.

"See. It's not just you. Other people blame me for not coming back. Not being at the funeral." She sighed. "I shouldn't have told Carol I'd stay."

"I told him to mind his own fucking business," Noah told her irritably. "Don't worry about him."

"You *what?* You said *that* to *Ron Larsen?* Noah! He's a deacon at St. Joseph's! He plays Santa Claus at the Winter Market every year! You can't talk that way to Santa Claus!"

He couldn't help a tiny little grin. "I might've used nicer words than that, but he got the message."

"Oh my god." She pinched the bridge of her nose. "Do not yell at old people on my behalf, okay?"

"What age would you consider the cut-off for 'old'?"

She looked up at him, trying to scowl, but losing the fight to a smile. "Noah. Don't yell at *anybody* on my behalf, alright?"

"Fine." He shrugged and continued onto his truck.

After a few steps, he doubled back. Ashlyn was in her front seat, about to pull her door shut, but he managed to grab the top.

"Hey, since you're still in town, you should come by sometime and take a look at your grandma's house. We've got all the rotten subfloor ripped out, and the rotten joists taken down. Dave—the plumber—should have the pipes done tomorrow."

Ashlyn considered him for a moment. . "Sure. It'll be interesting to see it all come together."

twelve

"THANK YOU, everyone, for being here tonight. As we get closer to the opening of this year's Winter Market, these meetings get more frequent, and we really appreciate everyone taking the time out of their busy schedules."

Carol Travers addressed the Winter Market planning committee, commercial partners, and volunteer contributors from the stage of the Lenora High School auditorium. It was a small auditorium with a small stage, but a crowd of at least fifty people was scattered throughout the seats.

"As many of you already know, John Richards has officially retired from his role as the Winter Market's financial manager. But, fortunately for us all, we have an immensely qualified accountant stepping in to fill his shoes. Ashlyn Vandale was born and raised right here in Lenora, and after quite a few years in Chicago as a *partner* at a major accounting firm—"

"*Junior* partner," Ashlyn muttered under her breath.

"—she's agreed to spend the holidays in Lenora to assist

with the Winter Market. Ashlyn? Where are you, honey? Stand up. Come on—stand up."

Reluctantly, Ashlyn rose from her auditorium seat, smiling uncomfortably at the other committee members.

"Let's all welcome Ashlyn with a round of applause."

Sitting beside her, Ruby Turner let out a wolf whistle as cheerful applause filled the auditorium. When it finally died away, Ashlyn sank gratefully into her seat. Ruby squeezed her arm affectionately.

"Thank you, Ashlyn," Carol said brightly. "Now, onto our first order of business. The holiday lights will go up the Saturday after Thanksgiving. Cole and Sons Electric is handling the—"

The heavy auditorium doors squealed as they swung open. The entire crowd turned to see Noah Sorenson standing in the doorway.

"Sorry," he said sheepishly, hurrying down the aisle.

"It's not really a committee meeting if Sorenson isn't late, hey?" someone called out.

A ripple of laughter followed the jibe.

Noah gave them a self-deprecating shrug and a smile, and ducked down into an open seat several rows up from Ashlyn.

"Alright," Carol said, slightly archly. "Now that all the market's commercial partners are here we can continue. We were discussing the holiday lights, which are part of your purview, Noah?"

"Yeah, me and four guys from my crew will be helping out."

"Good. So, as I was saying—"

"Excuse me!" Another woman's voice cut through Carol's. "Excuse me!"

Carol paused a second, looking up at the ceiling very

briefly, as though she might be discreetly begging God for strength. Looking back at the crowd with studied pleasantness, she said, "Yes, Debbie?"

"I submitted several proposals at our last meeting. The committee bylaws state that the committee has to address any submitted proposals and vote on them before any other business is conducted."

Another pause from Carol. She glanced at a different woman sitting in the front row. "Is that right, Michelle?" she asked quietly.

Michelle, making an apologetic face, nodded.

"Alright, then, Debbie. The committee discussed your proposals at the last meeting and it seemed like there was a clear consensus that—"

"But there was no vote!"

Carol let out a breath that bordered on a growl. "Fine. Michelle, do you have the proposals?"

Michelle nodded and handed up a folder. Carol flicked through the papers inside, her expression stony.

"Alright, let's vote then. Only committee members may vote, contributors who are not on the committee, please abstain. Proposal one: on replacing all the electric holiday street lights with candles, by a show of hands, who votes yes?"

A hand shot up in the back.

"Debbie," Carol said with terrifying politeness, "you are not a committee member. You are not eligible to vote."

With a huff, she withdrew her hand. Other than Debbie, not a single hand was raised.

"And who votes no?" Carol asked.

A dozen hands went up.

On the other side of the auditorium, Debbie huffed.

"Candlelight is more aesthetically aligned with the Winter Market's overall—"

"Sorry, Debbie. The council has voted. Your proposal has been rejected. Onto the next. Second proposal: requiring all Main Street businesses to maintain hot cocoa stations inside their premises for Winter Market guests. By a show of hands, who votes yes?"

Again, not a single hand was raised. One by one, five more proposals were struck down, followed each time by impatient outbursts from the thwarted Debbie.

Carol was finally able to move on to the topic of the holiday street decorations, but she'd only gotten as far as confirming that Sorenson Contracting and Cole & Sons Electric would be handling the set-up when another voice cut into Carol's. This time it was an older man, who stood up to address the meeting attendees as if he were making a State of the Union Address at the White House.

"What I don't understand, is why we're calling it the *Winter* Market. Back in my day, it was the *Christmas* Market, and nobody had a single problem with it. Now we can't say Christmas, anymore? Political correctness is ruining this town! Soon we won't be able to celebrate Christmas in our own homes!"

A small rumble of agreement supported him.

Carol took a deep breath, no longer disguising her struggle for composure. "Yes, thank you, Peter, for bringing that to our attention. As I've told you before, the name change was made twenty years ago to reflect the broader scope of vendors who participate in the market every year. Having a broader theme brings more vendors, more tourism, and more money to Lenora, while still leaving plenty of space for Christmas-themed vendors and performers. But, if you still want to change the market's name, then you need to submit a proposal for review by the committee."

"So it can get voted down?" Peter demanded, outraged.

"Most likely," Carol agreed. "Now, returning to the subject at hand—the street decorations."

The meeting continued with periodic interruptions from what Ashlyn could only conclude were incredibly bored lunatics. One woman wanted to move the Winter Market onto the lakeshore instead of Main Street—a suggestion she'd made multiple times before if Carol's reaction was anything to go by. One man wanted to change the rules for vendors to allow gambling stations, which Carol informed him was a violation of state law. Another man wanted to know why they didn't host the Winter Market in the summer when the weather was nicer. Yet another woman demanded to know—speaking as if the point hadn't been explicitly raised only thirty minutes before—why it wasn't called the Christmas Market anymore.

By the end of it, Carol looked ready to start beating people to death with her clipboard.

"And the last bit of news we have," she announced, eyeing the crowd as if daring someone else to pipe up, "is that Girard's has agreed to 'donate' the use of their parking lot for Winter Market guests. Which will greatly increase parking availability this year. Aiden will be updating our website with the new parking maps."

Ashlyn glanced over to see Aiden Sorenson sitting by himself on the opposite side of the auditorium. He nodded in recognition of Carol's announcement.

"Excellent. Then, I think that's it for tonight's meeting. Sorry it ran a little long, folks. The public meetings usually do. But thank you to everyone who came. Goodnight."

Ashlyn rose from her seat, with a sigh of relief. "Is every meeting like this?" she asked Ruby.

"No. When it's just the committee and the commercial partners, there's way less rabble-rousing. Most of the volunteers just enjoy participating. But a loud minority are here not because they really want to help out, but because they want to run things. And they think if they just make a rousing speech, the rest of us will rush to support them, and the committee will have no choice but to bow to their righteous demands."

"Great."

"Don't worry, there's only one more public meeting before the Market opens. The rest are just committee and partner meetings."

"Good." Ashlyn shrugged into her jacket and started for the aisle.

"Excuse me, Ashlyn?" A woman she vaguely recognized stopped her with a hand on her arm. She had a perfect blonde balayage, styled in shining waves around a soft face creased with smile lines. "Sorry, I don't know if you remember me. I'm Linda Moreau. I own the Icon Salon. Your grandma used to bring you there for your haircuts."

"Oh! I remember. Nice to see you again, Linda."

"You too, honey. It's been a long time. I was just wondering—Carol mentioned you're an accountant. Do you take on commercial clients?"

"That's all I do at my regular job, but my clients are generally large corporations."

Linda's face fell. "Ah. You're probably a little bit outside my budget then."

"Wait—no." Ashlyn wasn't sure what she was doing. Words just kept coming out of her mouth. "Who used to handle your accounts?"

"Well, I did. But I'm struggling with it, this year's taxes are a mess, and I don't need the IRS coming down on me, but John Richards retired, so I was just hoping—"

"You know what? Let me take a look at your books. I'm leaving after the New Year, so I won't be a long-term solution for you. But I can help out while I'm here." Managing the Winter Market's financials wouldn't take up very much of her time, especially since the system John had established was a tidy, well-oiled machine.

Linda's eyes widened. "Really? But, Ashlyn, I can't pay anything near what corporations are paying you—"

Ashlyn shrugged her concern away. "I'll talk to John and ask him how he charged clients before he retired. Whatever his rates were, I'll match. How's that sound?"

"Oh, Ashlyn, that's so— you're too sweet. Thank you so much."

"How about if I come by on Monday?"

"Yes! Perfect. Thank you!"

Ashlyn made her goodbyes to Linda and Ruby, and made her way out of the auditorium. She spied Noah and Aiden walking together further up the hall, and was immediately hit with a wave of deja vu. The last time she and Noah had been in these halls together, she'd been heartsick and pining over him.

And now here they were again, and she was… what, exactly? Attracted to him, yes. But did she know *this* Noah?

"Oh, hey, Ashlyn."

Without realizing it, she'd been hustling to catch up to him, and now he'd spotted her. "Oh, hey," she said, pretending she'd only just noticed him.

"You remember my brother Aiden?"

Aiden was a few years younger than Noah, but like all the Sorensons, he had bright blue eyes and raven dark hair.

He was thinner and a bit taller than Noah, his features a little more angular. His hair grew to his shoulders, but it looked more poetic than scruffy. Aiden had always had a slightly brooding quality to him that made him look like a Byronic anti-hero. In reality, he was a painfully shy sweetheart—or at least, he had been when Ashlyn had last known him.

"Of course I remember Aiden. We were both in chess club."

"Our school had a chess club?" Noah asked.

"Yes, and only cool people were allowed to join," Ashlyn told him before she turned her attention to his brother. "How've you been, Aiden? I heard you work with computers?"

"Hey, Ashlyn. I'm good. Yeah. Um, yeah, I'm a programmer for Domovoy."

"Domovoy? They're a client at my firm. Aren't they based in Chicago?"

"Yeah, but my position's remote. I could work from anywhere." His cheeks flushed and he looked away from her as if he'd admitted something embarrassing.

"That's awesome," Ashlyn said, trying to assuage whatever imaginary embarrassment he'd caused himself. "It's nice of you to donate your time and skills to the Winter Market."

Aiden shrugged. "Web design isn't really my thing, but I'm competent enough, I guess."

Noah snorted. "Competent? Come on, Aiden—admit you're a genius." He looked to Ashlyn. "He built a computer by himself when he was fourteen."

They reached the parking lot, and Noah held the door for Aiden and Ashlyn.

"It's actually not that difficult to build a computer,"

Aiden objected in his mild, self-effacing way. "The hardest thing at fourteen was saving up to buy the parts I needed."

"Shut up, Aiden," Noah said good-naturedly. "*I* wasn't building my own computer when I was fourteen."

"No, but you built a working go-cart and that pulley system we used to sneak stuff in and out of your bedroom window."

As Ashlyn listened to the two of them bickering over who was more impressive, a yawning pit of envy swallowed her heart. She'd never had that. She'd never felt like someone was 'on her side.' She'd always felt like she was fighting to prove her worthiness. At home. At school. At work. And it was never enough. She never reached the top. She'd never managed to do whatever it was that made people want to sing her praises the way the two Sorenson brothers did for each other.

"Okay, well, I'm parked over there," Ashlyn said, extricating herself from their conversation before her jealousy made her say something embarrassing. "See you guys later."

thirteen

WHEN ASHLYN PULLED up to her grandmother's house, two trucks were already parked in front. Neither was Noah's truck, but they had all the usual accouterments of a construction vehicle—ladders and buckets and diamond-stamped tool chests in the bed. She felt kind of weird walking into an active construction zone, but Noah had all but ordered her to stop by and check it out.

When she stepped inside, music blared from the kitchen, overlaid by the periodic snap of a nail gun. The front hall was completely gutted. The subfloor was all ripped up, open to the basement below, with beat-up sheets of plywood laid over the joists for walking. The side wall between the den and the hall was gone, with a makeshift support system holding up the ceiling made from rough-looking two-by-fours nailed together at even intervals.

It didn't really look like her grandma's house anymore. It was a relief. It was like walking into a blank slate.

"Hello?" Ashlyn called as she picked her way carefully over the plywood.

The music abruptly died in the kitchen. A young, lanky guy with cornrows and deep brown skin appeared in the doorway at the end of the hall. He was covered in plaster dust and wearing a long-sleeve t-shirt that said SORENSON CONTRACTING on the chest.

"Uh… hi?" he said, looking confused.

"Hi, sorry, I'm Ashlyn Vandale. I'm… the homeowner?"

At her doubtful tone, the confusion on his face deepened.

"I'm the homeowner," she said more firmly. "Noah told me to stop by and see how the work was coming along."

A second man appeared behind the first, this one pale, stocky, and red-haired. "Hi," he said gruffly. "Who're you?"

"She's the homeowner," the first man explained. "Says Sorenson told her to come see the progress."

The second man's brow furrowed. "He hates when clients come to worksites."

She didn't know what to say to that.

Fortunately, they both seemed to give up on trying to understand and just went along with it. "Well, most of what we've done so far is demo," the first guy said, gesturing at the gutted front hall. "But Dave finished the plumbing if you want to take a look at it?"

Ashlyn would have no idea what she was looking at. "You're working in the kitchen now?"

"Yeah. We got the plaster and sheetrock pulled off the ceiling and we're replacing the two rotted joists now." He turned and gestured for her to follow. The kitchen was covered in tarps, and the tarps were covered in gypsum and plaster dust. Overhead, she could see pipes and wires running between floor joists. The bathroom subfloor had been ripped out, allowing her to see into the space.

That blank slate feeling hit her again. It was a good one.

It felt like she was tearing out the rotten guts of her miserable childhood. She kind of wanted to tear out all the walls and floors and completely renovate the entire interior. Move the rooms around. Change everything. Make it an entirely different house.

"Looks good," Ashlyn said confidently, gazing around at all the wreckage.

"You work in construction?" the redhead asked her.

"No. It's just... it's good to see all the problems being ripped out."

The sound of the front door opening had all three of them swiveling towards the hall.

"How's it going in here?" Noah bellowed. He stepped into the kitchen and did a double-take at the sight of Ashlyn. "Oh, hey, Ash," he said in a decidedly more mellow tone. "Didn't see your car."

"I parked around the corner."

"Well," he glanced around. "What do you think?"

"I think it looks really good. Kind of makes me wish I'd made more changes."

Noah crossed his arms as he surveyed the progress. "Yeah? Like what?"

"I always hated the ugly carpeting in the living room. And I think the kitchen's really dated. And the dining room should have a wider doorway to the living room and smaller one to the kitchen—not the other way around. And I hate the wallpaper in pretty much every room."

Noah nodded, considering it. "We could rip up the living room carpet no problem. We're already putting down new flooring in so many parts of the house, it'd make sense to roll that in. The doorways on the dining room would be a little more complicated, but we could definitely do it. A kitchen remodel is beaucoup bucks, though. You might want to rethink that one. And the wallpaper... I mean, I can have my guys do it, but interior finishes like that aren't really in our usual wheelhouse..."

"No. I think I want to do it."

"What? All of it?"

"No—if you guys could pull up the living room carpet and fix the dining room doorways, I'll handle the rest."

Noah stared at her. "You're going to reno a kitchen on your own?"

She shrugged. "I'm not going to make it into a huge project. I'm just going to paint the cabinets and replace some fixtures. Just give it a facelift, you know?"

Noah shrugged. "That's a lot of work to do if you're just going to turn around and sell it."

"I know." She chewed her lip. "Maybe I won't bother."

"So where does that leave us on the living room flooring and the dining room doorways?"

"Do those," she said decisively.

He saluted her. "That'll change the estimate."

"I don't care. I never wanted this house. If I only break even after selling it, then that'll be fine."

Noah's brows raised, and he looked like he wanted to argue, but all he said was, "If you say so."

She nodded her confirmation. "Okay, well, thanks for letting me take a peek at the progress," she said to the other two guys. "I'll get out of your way now."

"I'll walk you to your car." Noah followed her out of the house. "You're happy with it?" he asked as he closed the front door behind him.

"Yeah. It's surprisingly therapeutic seeing it all torn up. Like an exorcism."

His brow creased, a faint line of worry as he looked at her. "Was she that bad?"

Ashlyn sighed, looking down at the sidewalk as they made their way to her car. "She never hit me or anything. She was just… unpleasant. All the time. Nothing I ever did was right. Chores were never done to her satisfaction. I didn't spend enough time studying. If I did anything that could be seen as 'fun,' I'd get yelled at and given more chores. Getting an A on something wasn't enough when I could've gotten an A plus. Being captain of a varsity team wasn't enough when we didn't have a winning record. Being valedictorian wasn't that impressive in such a small, rural school. When I did actually do something wrong, she came down on me like a hammer. Screaming and scolding and lecturing. Grounding me. Loading me up with chores until all I did all day was school, chores, and then sleep." It all came pouring out of her in an unstoppable rush. She was saying too much, but she couldn't stop. "If school interfered with church, I was in trouble. And if extracurriculars interfered with school, I was in trouble. But participating in all those extracurriculars—sports, debate team, the school newspaper, volunteering—"

She almost choked on the last one. Noah's gaze met hers, and while he looked troubled, there was a flash of recognition in his eyes.

"—I signed up for as much stuff as I could because it kept me out of the house. My goal was to only be there when I had to sleep."

"I'm sorry, Ash," he said roughly. "I wish I'd known."

Ashlyn shrugged, feeling suddenly drained. "You couldn't have done anything. You were a kid."

"I could've treated you better, at least."

A prickle of awareness ran over her skin. "I told you I had a massive crush on you," she said, striving for casual. "You must have treated me well enough."

"Do you know how badly I want to go back in time and beat the shit out of myself for being so oblivious?"

"You were my first kiss," Ashlyn blurted out. Immediately, she wished she could undo it.

Noah stared at her. "I—*what?*"

"Yep. Anyway, I have to go—" She turned to open her car door, but Noah's hand was on her shoulder, spinning her back around.

"*That* was your first kiss? When I left you in a closet thinking I hated you? Are you fucking kidding me?"

"Unfortunately, I'm not. But don't worry, I've had better since then."

A spark of something feral lit in Noah's gaze. "Oh, have you?"

Feeling like she was playing with fire, Ashlyn smiled sweetly. "Oh, yeah, way better. I almost forgot about yours until you reminded me."

"It's not really fair to compare a seventeen-year-old to more experienced competitors."

Ashlyn wrinkled her nose. "*Competitors?* Gross."

"You're the one who made it a competition. And I think it's only fair if I get a rematch."

Ashlyn almost choked on her tongue. "A rematch? Who else am I supposed to kiss for comparison?"

"Just use your memory." He stepped closer, caging her against the side of her car.

"Noah—" she said his name too breathily. It was basically an invitation.

He leaned closer, his piercing gaze holding hers. She couldn't breathe. She couldn't think.

"Hey, Sorenson!" one of his workers shouted, voice echoing from the front of the house.

Noah jerked away from her. They both stared at each other for a breathless moment.

"Sorenson!" the other guy shouted again. "Where are you?"

"That fucking guy," Noah muttered, stepping back from Ashlyn. He gave her a rueful grin. "I'll get that rematch, Ash."

Wide-eyed, she watched him walk back to the house. It wasn't until he was out of sight that she was able to peel herself off of the side of her car and get inside.

Fuck. She was in trouble.

fourteen

THE NEXT WINTER Market meeting was in the high school auditorium again, but since it wasn't a public meeting, the crowd was less than half of the last meeting. Ruby was there again, as a commercial partner, so Ashlyn slid into the seat next to her.

The meeting started with a notably less frazzled-looking Carol. "Thank you to our committee members and commercial partners for being here tonight. "We'll start with a financial report from our new financial manager."

Ashlyn stood up and turned to face most of the auditorium. "We're in good shape," she said, automatically slipping into the professional voice she used with clients. "John was running a really tight ship, so everything is on track." She ran through a quick list of recent payments to outside contractors, which wasn't terribly high yet. "There'll obviously be more to discuss when we get closer to the opening of the market, but everything's looking good."

"Thank you, Ashlyn. Next order of business, we are still missing—"

The auditorium doors swung open, and in strode Noah. He waved sheepishly at everybody as he hurried to duck into a seat.

"Jesus Christ, Sorenson," Adam Cole complained. "Up your meds, or something."

Noah flipped him the bird, hiding it behind his lapel from Carol and most of the other committee members. Adam rolled his eyes, crossing his arms as he returned his attention to Carol.

"Nice to have you with us, Noah," Carol said, sounding mildly annoyed. "Anyways, as I was saying…"

The meeting was shorter and less volatile than the last one. Ashlyn half-listened to the committee members as they discussed plans, while a small part of her brain was wondering what Adam meant when he told Noah to "up his meds."

When the meeting was over, Ashlyn walked out to her car a few yards behind Noah. She wanted to ask him about Adam's comment—but the demand he'd made a few days ago for a "rematch" had her feeling ridiculously shy. She wasn't sure what she wanted. She'd been single for so long, she wanted it almost too much. Especially from Noah Sorenson. But that was exactly the problem. He was *Noah Sorenson.* How could she just blithely kiss him and then carry on with her life? She'd tried it once and it had been a mess.

While she was quibbling, Noah glanced back and caught sight of her. He smiled and fell back to walk with her.

"Hey, Ash," he greeted her easily, as if the last time they saw each other he hadn't had her pressed against her car, with his mouth bare inches away from hers.

"Hey." Desperate to turn her brain down some other avenue, she asked, "What did Adam mean when he told you to 'up your meds'?"

Noah's affable expression briefly flickered with annoyance. "He meant Adderall. I take it for ADHD."

"You do?" That... made a lot of sense, actually.

"Yeah. Didn't figure it out until well after high school, unfortunately. Who knows what I could've done with myself if I'd caught it sooner." He said it lightly, but Ashlyn sensed old grief in the words.

"You're a successful business owner. I think you turned out alright," she said, matching his tone.

He shrugged. "Anyway, I take it first thing in the morning. By the end of the workday, it's worn off. I get a little more scattered after that."

"Oh."

He glanced over at her. "Rethinking everything you know about me?"

"No. More like... fitting a missing puzzle piece into place."

He smiled. "It makes sense, doesn't it? I can't believe it took me so long to figure it out. I wouldn't have even gotten tested for it if an old boss hadn't suggested it to me."

"Your parents never thought about it?"

"They had six kids. As long as one of us wasn't actively dying, their attention was usually a little divided."

As opposed to Ashlyn's childhood, which had been marked by a spotlight of constant, brutally intense scrutiny.

"Ashlyn?"

She startled as an unexpected voice came from behind her. Turning, she found herself facing Jeremy Wagner, the owner of Wagner's Electronics. He was about a decade older than Ashlyn and Noah, and had taken over ownership his father's electronics store shortly before Ashlyn had left Lenora. His dark hair was suspiciously free of grays, though the corners of his eyes were creased with smile lines.

"Sorry to interrupt you," he said. "I don't know if you remember me. I'm Jeremy—"

"Wagner," Ashlyn finished for him. "I remember you. How are you?"

"Not bad. I just wanted to ask—Linda Moreau mentioned that you were helping her with her taxes this year. I was wondering if you were taking on other clients. After John retired, I went to this online service, but they're absolutely awful. I don't really trust them, and I was wondering if you had the time to take a look at the numbers for me?"

Ashlyn hesitated. Between the Winter Market and Linda's taxes, she wasn't exactly working a full-time job. And while she was enjoying catching up with her old friends, there were only so many hours she could fill with lunch meet-ups and kaffeeklatsches. She could easily take on another client. But she wasn't staying, and she didn't want to give people the impression that she was.

"Um…"

"It's fine if you can't," Jeremy said quickly. "I just thought I'd ask."

"The thing is, I'm headed back to Chicago after the new year, back to my regular job, so I won't be able to offer my services beyond that. But if you just need somebody to take a look at what you've got so far…"

Jeremy nodded enthusiastically.

"Okay, well, I can do that, then. Do you have time to meet with me tomorrow?"

"Yes, that'd be perfect. Would first thing in the morning work for you?"

"Sure." Ashlyn held out her hand to shake. "See you tomorrow, Jeremy."

"Thank you so much. Have a good night." Jeremy

walked off towards his vehicle, leaving Noah and Ashlyn alone again.

"Lenora's prodigal sweetheart has returned to save the day." Noah mused.

"I'm not the prodigal sweetheart. I'm the heartless bitch who abandoned her saintly grandmother. Get it straight, Sorenson."

"Well, I bet you do taxes better than Judy Vandale's corpse can."

Ashlyn gasped in shock.

"Too far?"

A scandalized giggle escaped her. "Yes! And I'm going to hell for laughing at that."

They reached her car, and Noah stood by as she unlocked it and got inside. Before she could swing the door shut, he caught the top of it. "I'm still waiting on that rematch, Princess."

And then he closed her door and sauntered off. Ashlyn stared after him, flushed with both annoyance and want.

fifteen

WORK HAD SLOWED DOWN at the resort while Wes fought to figure out who was behind the shady shell corp that owned the portion along the lakeshore. It was nice to see the place his grandparents had once owned being brought back to life, but Noah had his doubts as to whether Wes would ever manage to buy back the shorefront property. Whoever was behind Fortuna Property Investments seemed to take malicious pleasure in shutting down all of Wes's attempts at negotiation.

So, while Wes spun his wheels with the resort, Noah turned his attention to his other projects. With the resort on the back burner, he had his crew split onto three different jobs. If any of them needed more bodies, it was probably the eight-unit apartment building on the north side of town. Instead, he found himself driving south, to the late Judy Vandale's house.

Inside, he found Jake and Anton framing in the new hallway wall. The floors all had new subfloor laid, ready and waiting for flooring, and the living room's green shag carpeting had been ripped up to reveal pristine maple strip flooring underneath.

"Hey, Sorenson," Jake greeted him, holding a two-by-four in place as Anton drove in several screws. Both guys were meticulous framers, which was why Noah had put them on Ashlyn's house.

"Hey, guys. Things are coming along nicely here."

"'Course they are," Jake said. "You got me on the job, don't you?"

"How's the upstairs bathroom look?"

"Subfloor's all cut, just needs to be anchored down."

"I'll take care of it," he told them, heading back out to the truck to grab his tools.

An hour later, he was putting the final screw into the new bathroom subfloor.

"Hey, Noah."

He jumped, managing to crack his head on the underside of the pedestal sink, then swore viciously as he clutched his head. He swiveled to find Ashlyn standing in the bathroom doorway, wide-eyed.

"I didn't mean to startle you," she said quickly. "I figured you heard me stomping up the stairs..."

"It's not your fault." He rubbed the tender spot on his skull as he got to his feet. "Did you come by to see the progress?"

"Sort of. I was actually planning to start taking down all the wallpaper. I bought a steamer and everything." She held up a shopping bag. "So... I'll just be downstairs, then."

He realized Ashlyn was looking anywhere but directly at him, and it took him a second to remember that the last two times he'd seen her, he'd told her he wanted to kiss her.

106

Probably not a wise idea, considering she was leaving town forever in a few weeks, but he had terrible impulse control. Amphetamines could curb it, but couldn't completely eradicate it. He couldn't really blame the ADHD for this one, though. He'd always been reckless when it came to Ashlyn. Dense, but reckless.

"Do you want help?"

She hesitated. "You said you don't typically do this sort of thing."

"It wouldn't be part of the job. I just meant… as a friend."

"Oh." She hesitated, an obvious internal debate being waged.

For fuck's sake, why'd he have to run his big fucking mouth about kissing her? Now everything was weird and Ashlyn was uncomfortable and—

"Yeah, alright. Thanks."

He didn't react right away. "Yeah?" he echoed.

She nodded. "I'm starting in the living room, but my plan is to take *all* the wallpaper down in the entire house and repaint all the walls."

Noah followed her downstairs. "That's a big job."

She shrugged. "I've got the time."

Taking the wallpaper down turned out to be relatively easy with the steamer. Noah got the seven-foot ladder from his truck, and working together, they managed to strip three of the living room walls before Jake and Anton popped their heads in to let him know they were leaving.

"Should we call it a day?" Noah asked Ashlyn.

She frowned at the last wall still covered in dark, busy, floral wallpaper. "You go, you worked all day."

He brought the ladder over to the last wall. "Nah, let's get this one finished and then we'll call it."

Ashlyn hesitated. "You've been helping me for hours. I feel like I should pay you."

"Order a pizza and we'll be square."

She smiled. "Wow, cheap date."

THEY WERE HALFWAY DONE WITH THE LAST LIVING ROOM wall when the pizza arrived. They sat on the floor to eat in companionable silence. Noah had just bit into his second slice when Ashlyn said, "When are you going to kiss me?"

He froze, pizza in mouth.

"I'm just wondering."

Noah chewed slowly, buying time while he figured out what to say. He'd forgotten how blunt she could be. When they were kids, that bluntness had occasionally been devastating, but mostly he'd liked it. He generally preferred straightforwardness over coyness.

"Are you saying you want me to?" he finally asked.

"I don't know." Her face was as blank as it'd been that day in the food pantry's supply closet, but he forced himself not to take it for rejection this time. Blunt she may be, but that didn't mean Ashlyn wore her heart on her sleeve.

"Then I'll just have to spring it on you, so you can figure it out," he said, giving into the recklessness.

"What, right now?"

"Considering we both just ate a pizza covered in onions, peppers, and garlic, I'll save it for another day?"

"Which day?"

"That's for me to know and you to find out."

She scowled at him, but it was an expression he recognized. Annoyance and affection. She wasn't the only person who gave him that look—his parents and siblings came to mind—but the sight of Ashlyn Vandale trying to frown at him when she obviously wanted to smile was burned into his brain. He'd loved provoking her when they were teenagers. It'd been an obsessive game of his—tease her until she was irritated, then keep teasing until it turned into laughter. She'd always been so serious, even as a kid. Getting a laugh out of her had been like winning an award.

After a moment of comfortable silence, Ashlyn said, "I'm leaving after Christmas."

"I know."

"I just..." She stared down at the slice of pizza in her hand. "I've built a whole life for myself away from here."

"I know."

"And I have to go back to that life. This is just... a break."

"I don't have any expectations, Princess."

The thoughtful bleakness fell off of her face as she bristled.

Before she could tear him a new one for that old nickname, he said, "It was never an insult, Ash. Not from me."

Her prickliness subsided, though she looked skeptical.

"What's that saying?" He looked up, trying to remember. "'Truth in jest,'" he recalled, looking back at her. "I acted like it was a joke, but..." He shrugged.

She looked totally disarmed by his words. "Noah," she said faintly.

He gave her a smile that felt ill-fitting on his face and shrugged again. "Just thought you should know."

sixteen

AT THE NEXT meeting for the Winter Market, Noah was actually on time. But that was probably because he'd been helping Ashlyn take down the wallpaper in the kitchen of her grandma's house, and she'd stopped and told him they needed to head over for the meeting. He'd been so focused on the task at hand, she'd had to say his name twice to get his attention.

They sat next to each during the meeting and walked out together afterwards. The conversation that they didn't *quite* have about what exactly was going on between them had been hovering in the air for the past few days. While Noah seemed content to let it stew, Ashlyn couldn't bear the tension. Uncharacteristically for her, though, she was avoiding bringing it up again. Talking it out had a sense of finality that she wasn't ready for.

"I want the new flooring to match the living room floors," she blurted out as they walked back to their vehicles, mostly to keep herself from blurting out more emotionally volatile words. It wasn't completely a dodge, though. She had been thinking about the house a lot. Changing the house from the prison it used to be into a safe place, a new place, was therapeutic. Or maybe addictive. Every time she made one change, she thought of another. She wanted to see the house as it could have been—as it should have been. Making the house clean and beautiful felt like she was renovating the past, in a way.

Noah's brow furrowed as he considered what she said. "I think those floors are original to the house. Modern maple—"

"I know, modern flooring isn't going to match right. But I saw this home renovation show where—"

Noah groaned.

"What?"

"Those fucking shows are the bane of my existence. They do shit that looks good on camera—not what's actually functional."

"Oh." Ashlyn chewed her lip.

"Wait, sorry. Ignore that." Noah scrubbed at his jaw, fingers rasping over beard. "I wouldn't usually say it that way to a client. Tell me what you had in mind and I'll tell you if it's doable."

"I thought we could maybe find salvaged flooring? There are two different salvage warehouses within an hour's drive of Lenora. I called the one in Grand Junction, and they said they had loads of old maple strip flooring."

"But is it usable? That's the problem." He thought for a second. "I'd have to take a look at it. If it's in good condition, then we could do it. But if it's in rough condition—and I'm guessing it is—we could probably still work with it, but it'll end up looking like shit, no matter how careful we are. You can only refinish that old maple strip so many times."

"Oh." She considered her options for a moment. "Well,

I was going to go take a look this weekend. What if I sent you pictures of it? Could you decide if it's usable?"

He shook his head. "I'd want to see it in person. I can go with you."

"On the weekend?"

"Sure."

"What do you charge for consults?"

He shook his head, giving her a lazy smile. "Buy me lunch."

The pragmatic side of her brain was hesitant, but the lonely side spoke too quickly, "Alright. Thanks. Saturday?"

He nodded. "I'll pick you up from the Hideaway at nine."

"No, I can drive."

"But I have a pickup and a trailer. If you want the flooring, we'll need to haul it back."

"Okay, but I'm paying for gas."

Noah nodded. "Sounds like a deal. See you Saturday."

ASHLYN SAT AT A TABLE BY THE WINDOWS IN THE Hideaway's diner, sipping coffee while she waited for Noah. When he finally pulled up, he was ten minutes late. He jumped out of his truck, looking frazzled as he hurried into the diner. He spotted her at her table and rushed over.

"I'm sorry, Ash," he said quickly. "I forgot to set an alarm for today."

"Do you usually sleep in on weekends? We could've gone later in the day."

"No—I always set alarms for appointments, meetings, dates... er... that sort of thing. If it's out of my usual routine, I won't remember it without an alarm."

"Oh. Well." She was still hung up on *date.* "You remembered anyway."

Noah's brow was furrowed, his whole body uneasy with guilt.

"Don't worry about it. I was enjoying my coffee." She put a few dollars on the table and got up. "Ready to go?"

She really had been enjoying her coffee and watching the sedate traffic along Main Street. Noah's lateness really didn't bother her. Her childhood had been so heavily regimented. Her life on her own continued to be highly controlled because in the early days, a mistake would've meant she had to go crawling back to her grandma for help. Eventually, living that way just became a habit rather than a necessity. It was kind of a relief to just go with the flow and not care about timing.

She realized she was actually slightly dreading returning to her life in Chicago because she was enjoying the pace of life in Lenora—helping a few local businesses on her own schedule and doing whatever she wanted with her free time.

"Really, I'm sorry, Ash. It's not because I don't give a shit. It's—"

She laid a hand on his arm. "Seriously, it's not a big deal. Let's go."

He clenched his jaw, nodded, and pulled the door open for her.

"WE CAN USE THESE," NOAH SAID, SOUNDING STUNNED AS he examined the old floorboards.

"Really?" Ash asked, excitedly.

Noah nodded, his gaze intent as he flipped over a few more boards, examining them.

"They came from the old Verstecken Brewery—the one

they tore down in Clearwater," the owner of the warehouse, a portly older man named Kevin, explained. "We got thousands of square feet of the stuff,"

Noah pulled out his phone, looking up some notes he had made for himself. "We'll need seven hundred square feet, minimum." He glanced Ashlyn. "You want to do the kitchen in tile or hardwood?"

"Hardwood."

"Nine hundred, then. And then a bit more, to be safe. Say, a thousand?"

"Okay," Ashlyn agreed.

Kevin chuckled. "Boy, if only me and my wife agreed so easily. You must be newlyweds."

"Oh, um—" Ashlyn felt her cheeks flushing.

"We're not married," Noah said, sounding as awkward as Ashlyn felt.

"I'm his—"

"Friend," Noah said at the same time as Ashlyn said, "client."

They both looked at each other.

Kevin cleared his throat, very obviously fighting for a straight face. "Right, then. Let's ring you up, I'll have my boys start loading your trailer."

"Um, actually," Ashlyn cut in. "I wanted to replace the kitchen counters, too. I was wondering if you had any salvaged butcher block counters?"

"You want the counters taken out?" Noah asked, sounding concerned.

"I can do it. It's not that hard."

"They're heavy," he said dubiously. "And you'll need help installing the new ones."

"I'll figure it out."

He gave her a skeptical look. "Make this easier for both

of us, Ashlyn, and ask me to help, otherwise I'm going to have to bully my way into it."

"I can't ask you to help with this. You're helping with too much as it is!"

He stared at her flatly.

"*Noah.*"

He continued to stare.

A soft, light feeling ate away at her pride. She sighed. "Fine. Would you help me with the counters?"

His flat stare turned into an affable smile. "Happy to." He looked to Kevin. "Got any salvaged butcher block?"

THE DRIVE BACK TO LENORA WAS UNEVENTFUL, AND NOAH went along with Ashlyn's bland small talk while she desperately avoided the topic of all the help he was giving her and The Kiss and the fact that she was leaving in a month and a half.

"So, what are your Thanksgiving plans?" she asked. It was an innocuous question she asked any number of coworkers every year, but it hit her suddenly that she'd be spending the holiday alone. She usually did. But being in Lenora and still alone for the holidays made her stomach feel hollow, her heart leaden. She had been trying to escape that when she'd taken her leave of absence.

"My parents always host, so I'll be at their place. What about you?"

"Um…"

Noah's phone buzzed in the center console, sparing her from having to say out loud how lonely and pathetic she was.

"Sorry—it's my mom. One second." He picked up the phone. "Hey, Mom. What's up?" A pause as he listened.

"I'm about a half hour away, but I have to drop off—nope, okay, okay, hang on. Yeah, I hear you. Hang on." He pulled the phone away from his face. To Ashlyn, he asked, "Do you mind if I swing by my parents' place before I drop you off? There's a problem with their furnace and the whole house is apparently freezing."

"Of course I don't mind," Ashlyn said quickly.

Noah brought the phone back to his ear. "I'll be there in half an hour."

"I didn't know you did HVAC stuff, too," Ashlyn said when he hung up.

"I don't. Not professionally, anyway. But my dad will try to fix it himself if I don't do it, and the last time my dad messed with the furnace, they had to clear out of the house in the middle of the night because of a carbon monoxide leak." With a grim expression, he tightened his hands on the wheel.

seventeen

THEY REACHED HIS PARENTS' house in slightly less than a half hour. The Sorensons lived in a sprawling log-sided house with a stone chimney, deep in the woods a few minutes outside of Lenora. Noah let Ashlyn in through the garage, leading her down a small hallway into the kitchen where Renee Sorenson was calmly chopping veggies while wearing a knitted wool hat and her winter coat.

"Jesus, Mom, it can't be more than fifty degrees in here. Why didn't you call sooner?"

Renee had the same raven black hair as all her children, though hers was heavily streaked with silver. Her eyes were a stormy gray, the corners creased from years of laughter and smiles.

"I was out running errands. I only got home a few minutes before I called you. It must've gone out while I was gone."

"Was it working this morning?"

"As far as I could tell," Renee answered placidly, quartering potatoes and dropping them into a kettle.

"Alright, I'm going to go take a look. Hopefully it's just the pilot light."

He started to walk away, but Ashlyn cleared her throat nervously and he swung back around.

"Mom, this is Ashlyn Vandale. I'm working on a house renovation for her." He threw an arm around Ashlyn's shoulders and shepherded her over to the dining area on the other side of the kitchen counter.

Renee looked up from her cutting board, looking at Ashlyn for a moment with a furrowed brow before recognition dawned. "Oh, Ashlyn! Judy's granddaughter. I remember you. Have a seat, honey. I have a pot of coffee on, would you like a cup?"

"That sounds great, thank you. It's nice to see you again, Mrs. Sorenson."

"Psh. Call me Renee." She bustled around the counter with a mug and a half-full coffee carafe. "Creamer? We have French vanilla and caramel creme."

"French vanilla please."

Renee bustled to the fridge, then returned to the table with the creamer and her own coffee cup, settling into the seat across from Ashlyn.

"So, what have you been up to, hon?" Renee asked brightly. "I thought I heard you were living in some big city. Minneapolis?"

"Chicago, actually. I've been working as an accountant at a firm that does external audits for other companies." God, she wished there were a way to make that sound less mind-numbing.

"Oooh, big city girl," Renee mused. "How exciting! I suppose you're back in Lenora because of your grandma. Sorry for your loss."

"Yeah, I came up to settle her estate," Ashlyn said,

glazing past the condolences. "The house is in rough shape, so Noah's getting it fixed up so I can sell it."

"So you're not staying then? I thought maybe—" Her gaze flashed to the doorway Noah had disappeared through. "Well, never mind. It's nice to see Noah being social, though. He's been a bit of a hermit. What were you two up to today?"

Their relationship had straddled some strange line between professional and not-at-all professional, and Ashlyn didn't know how to begin explaining why she was spending Saturday hanging out with Noah at a salvage warehouse. It would require admitting that Noah was helping her do some of the renovations without pay, which made things seem more... unprofessional between them than she should really be allowing. But if she didn't explain that, his mom would think they were hanging out purely for the sake of each others' company and that was... too much.

"Um. I went with Noah to pick up some flooring for my grandma's house." There. Succinct, but vague. Renee didn't need to know that Noah had volunteered to join her and that she'd been spending most of the day wondering if and when he was going to kiss her.

"On a Saturday?" Renee shook her head. "I knew he was overworking himself again."

Shit. Now she had to say something. "No, it's—uh... off the clock, I guess?"

Renee considered that, a gleam of interest in her eyes. "Oh?"

"I was going to go by myself, but Noah offered to come. Like, professionally. But also... not like, *working* working."

The interested gleam intensified. "Hmmm." She sipped her coffee. "So, what are your Thanksgiving plans?"

"I don't have any," Ashlyn said, well aware that she was walking straight into a trap.

"Oh, no! Really? Well, we can't have that. Why don't you come here for Thanksgiving?"

"I don't want to intrude on your family," Ashlyn tried to demur.

Renee was one of those sweet but steely people who were impossible to defy. "It's not intruding! The more the merrier! You have to come, honey. There'll be too much, food—there always is—so really, you'd be doing me a favor. And, besides, I won't be able to enjoy the day if I know you're all by yourself. Say you'll come."

"Ah, well… alright. I— well. Thank you for the invitation. What can I bring?"

"Bring to what?" Noah asked as he walked back into the kitchen.

"Good news!" Renee announced cheerfully. "Ashlyn's going to join us for Thanksgiving!"

Noah looked blank with surprise for a second, but he quickly recovered with a smile. "I should've thought of that. I guess I just assumed with all your friends, you'd be going to one of theirs."

"Nope." She'd been too embarrassed to ask, and everyone else probably also assumed she already had plans.

"Their loss is our gain," Renee said, patting Ashlyn's hand.

Noah went to the sink and washed his hands. "It's the pilot light. I think you should just replace that whole furnace. That thing is thirty years old."

Renee sighed. "You know your father."

Noah nodded. "Alright, well, I have to run to the hardware store to get a new pilot assembly—and I need to get

Ashlyn back to her place. Why don't you go to Aunt Lisa's so you don't freeze?"

Renee shook her head. "I have to finish getting dinner ready. I'll live."

Noah looked like he wanted to argue, but he must have thought it futile because he turned his attention to Ashlyn. "Thanks for waiting. Ready to go?"

She nodded. "Thanks for the coffee, Renee. See you on Thursday."

"Can't wait! Bye, Ashlyn."

eighteen

THE SORENSON HOUSE was absolutely slammed with people when Ashlyn arrived. A lot of them had straight black hair and light-colored eyes, but there were several brunettes and at least one blonde in the gathering. To Ashlyn's immense relief, Noah was the one to answer the door when she rang the bell. His mother appeared just behind him, shouldering him out of the way so she could hug Ashlyn.

"Ashlyn! Welcome! Ooh, what's this?" She drew back, examining the tray in Ashlyn's hands. She'd bought two-dozen mini onion tartlets from the fancy deli at Girard's. "I told you you didn't need to bring anything! But these look delicious, bring them to the kitchen, we'll find room on the counter."

Noah trailed behind as his mother swept her away.

"Ian! Ian!" Renee brought Ashlyn up short in front of her husband, Ian Sorenson. "This is Ashlyn. Do you remember her? She was a friend of Noah's back when they were kids."

Ian's eyes were as crystalline blue as all his kids', but he had lighter hair. It had probably once been a fawn brown, but had gone mostly silver now. His facial features were similar to Noah's, except twenty-some years older, and clean-shaven.

"Hi, honey. Nice to have you with us." Ashlyn doubted he recognized her, but his smile seemed genuine as he welcomed her.

Renee swept Ashlyn onward. In the kitchen, she got Ashlyn a glass of wine and urged her to try various hors d'oeuvres. By the time something else called Renee's attention, Ashlyn had a little plate filled with cocktail sausages, ham and pickle roll-ups, shrimp cocktail, Swedish meatballs, spinach puffs, and a bacon-wrapped jalapeno popper.

"Your mother is a force of nature," Ashlyn told Noah as she watched Renee hurry over to the oven to check on the turkey.

Before Noah could respond, his brother Wes appeared beside him, smiling at Ashlyn and offering her a friendly, one-armed hug.

"Hey, Ashlyn. Mom mentioned she invited you." He gave Noah a significant glance. Noah scowled at him.

"What?" Ashlyn asked.

"What?" Wes said innocently.

"What was that secret little sibling telepathy conversation, there?" she pressed.

"You're an only child. How do you know about sibling telepathy?" Wes joked. Before Ashlyn could point at that he'd dodged the question, he changed the topic. "I heard you're on the Winter Market planning committee."

"Wha—oh. Yeah. John Richards wanted to step back from it."

123

"I also heard that you're Jeremy Wagner's new accountant."

"Well, just temporarily, while I'm here."

"And how long is that?"

"I'm leav—" She had to clear a suddenly dry throat. "I'm leaving after Christmas."

"Too bad. I know a lot of people would love it if you stayed." He glanced at Noah again. Noah shot him a warning look.

Ashlyn felt her cheeks heating. "I—"

"Oh, hey, it's snowing." Wes nodded to the kitchen patio doors, where fat, gentle snowflakes drifted down in the glow of the outside lights. "Anyways, I'm going to get something to drink. Nice having you here, Ashlyn." He squeezed her shoulder, then moved on.

Noah and Ashlyn looked at each other.

"Happy Thanksgiving?" Ashlyn said uncomfortably.

Noah regarded her inscrutably for a moment. Just as he seemed like he was going to say something, an older man swooped in, clapping Noah heartily on the back.

"Hey, Uncle Jeff."

"Who's the girlfriend, Noah? You should be introducing her."

"Oh—" Ashlyn straightened. We're not—"

"She's not—"

An older woman appeared beside Ashlyn. "Who's this, Noah? Why haven't you introduced us to your girlfriend?"

"Aunt Gina, Ashlyn's not—"

"*Noah's* got a *girlfriend?*" A woman close in age to Ashlyn inquired merrily, eyes wide with excitement.

Someone else turned around. "He does?"

"Introduce us!" chimed in another voice.

"SHE'S NOT MY GIRLFRIEND!" Noah barked.

"Noah!" Renee chided, a steaming pan of roasted brussels sprouts in her hands. "Inside voice!"

Noah scrubbed at his face. "This is Ashlyn," he said in a determinedly measured voice. "She's an old friend from school. She's only in town for a few weeks. She is *not* my girlfriend."

"Shame," his Uncle Jeff said. "Welp. I need another drink. Nice meeting you Ashley."

"Ashlyn," she muttered as the rest of the onlookers dispersed, interest lost.

"Sorry about that," Noah said.

In the deflated quiet, Noah's brother Aiden passed by.

"Hi Ashlyn," he greeted her in his characteristically soft-spoken way, with only the briefest flash of eye contact before he looked away.

"Hey, Aiden. How've you been?"

"Not bad," he answered as he walked on by, opening the patio door and slipping outside.

"He's not trying to be rude," Noah said quietly. "He really hates crowds. This is torture for him."

"I'm not offended. It is really crowded in here. Is this all your family?"

"Yeah. My mom has seven brothers and sisters, my dad has five. I don't actually even know how many cousins I have. Thirty? And a bunch of them are married, and at least half of them have kids now…" He gazed around at the happy chaos.

Ashlyn followed his gaze, feeling a pang of melancholy. Noah's family was so close with each other, so happy to see each other. She couldn't imagine what that was like. She felt a bit like a starving child standing outside a bakery window. She felt like an intruder, even though she'd been invited. She didn't know anyone there except Noah. And the fact that she *wasn't* his girlfriend meant that she really didn't belong here—his mother had invited her out of pity.

"What's wrong?" Noah asked, interrupting her maudlin thoughts.

"Nothing."

He gave her a look but didn't press. Instead, he said, "Come with me."

She followed Noah out of the kitchen, past the living room, and down a carpeted hallway to the very end. The half-ajar door opened to reveal a family room of sorts. There were two big, floral sofas that looked at least thirty years old. There was an older TV hooked up to a classic Nintendo with two twenty- or thirty-something guys playing Super Mario Bros. A round card table set up behind the couches had four of its six folding chairs occupied by people playing a card game.

"Hey guys, this is Ashlyn. Ash, these are my cousins— Leo, Jenny, Dan, and Emma."

The cousins ranged in age from early twenties to early forties. Leo and Jenny had the characteristic Sorenson black hair, while Dan had dark brown hair peppered with gray, and Emma's hair was bleached bone-white with teal-colored ends. Dan, who looked to be the eldest, gestured to their in-progress game. "We just started. We can re-deal if you want to play. It's 500 rummy."

"Deal us in," Noah said, pulling out a seat for Ashlyn, and then taking the one next to her.

"Kids, dinner's ready," Renee called, leaning into the room with a smile.

Ashlyn looked up, wondering when kids had come into the room, before realizing that Renee Sorenson was referring to all the twenty-, thirty-, and forty-somethings as "kids." Which made sense, considering at least one of them was her own kid. But nobody had called Ashlyn a kid in an incredibly long time. She hadn't felt like a kid for an even longer time.

But she'd had fun with Noah's cousins. That trespasser feeling had faded, and she'd found herself trading trash talk with Leo and Emma like they were old friends. It felt good to be considered one of them—one of "the kids."

Riding that contented feeling, Ashlyn followed Noah and the others out to the kitchen, where the counters were heaped with food and crowded with people filling their plates. The older folks and the smaller children had all already gotten theirs and sat positioned around the house at various folding tables and other makeshift surfaces.

When Ashlyn reached the counter, she filled her plate with a little bit of everything and then followed Noah back to the game room.

"So, how long have you two been together?" Jenny asked as she sat down, gesturing to Noah and Ashlyn.

"WE'RE NOT TOGETHER," Noah growled.

Jenny's eyes went wide and she pressed her lips tightly together as if fighting a smile.

"There was a lot of rage behind that denial," Dan observed with a smirk. "Sounds like there's more to it than that."

"There's nothing to it," Noah said flatly.

"We're not together," Ashlyn put in, more calmly. "I'm only in town for a few weeks. Noah and I were—friends in high school." She kept talking to hopefully smooth over her slight falter. "His mom only invited me out of pity."

"It wasn't pity," Aiden said mildly as he stepped into the room.

127

"Shut up, Aiden," Noah growled.

Aiden shrugged and took a seat on one of the couches.

Ashlyn looked to Noah with a questioning frown. "What—"

"Don't eat the potato salad," Noah interrupted her.

She looked down at the helping on her plate. It looked perfectly ordinary.

"My Aunt Beth made it. She makes it every year. And every year, it's an abomination," he explained. "We all take a scoop because nobody wants to hurt her feelings. But you have to mash it around with your other leftovers when you're done. Don't actually eat it."

"Oh, god," Leo groaned. "Remember last year? She put black olives and raisins in it. A *lot* of raisins."

"No, that was two years ago," Jenny said grimly. "Last year was when she added crushed corn chips 'for texture'."

"That one wasn't so bad," Emma said. "Remember when she put whole cloves of raw garlic in it? You couldn't even pick them out because they blended in with the potatoes and eggs." She shuddered.

"Yeah, but the worse one was when she replaced the mayo with her homemade 'aioli'."

Everyone shuddered.

"Aioli sounds good," Ashlyn ventured.

"Yeah, I'm sure would be if Aunt Beth actually knew *how* to make aioli," Dan said with a distant look of remembered trauma.

"What was even in it?" Jenny asked, grimacing.

"I don't want to know," Emma decided. The others seemed to agree.

Ashlyn looked down at her plate. "Okay, well, to be perfectly honest, I'm now morbidly curious to taste this potato salad."

"Don't!" the entire room objected.

"I have to." She picked up a small bit with her fork.

"I can't look." Emma covered her face.

Ashlyn put it in her mouth. She chewed for a bit, pondered, then shrugged. "It just tastes like ordinary potato salad."

"Are you serious?" Leo asked.

"Yeah." She scooped up another forkful. "Maybe she bought it at a deli."

Shocked, the others quickly moved to try it. A second later, they were spitting it out on their plates, coughing and groaning in revulsion.

"What the fuck did we ever do to you?" Dan demanded, wounded.

Ashlyn laughed, reaching for her wine glass to finally wash the awful taste out of her mouth. It was horribly bitter and had a burn like the hottest horseradish.

"Your girlfriend is a menace," Emma told Noah, wiping at her tongue with her napkin.

"She's not my girlfriend," Noah said impatiently. "But she's always been a menace."

Ashlyn shot him a half-hearted scowl. He grinned back at her. Her gaze fell to his plate, where his potato salad was untouched. "You didn't try it?"

Noah's grin grew. "I could tell you were fucking with them."

"How?" she demanded.

He shrugged. "I don't know. I could just tell. Nice job, by the way."

"*Awww,*" Jenny cooed. "What a cute not-couple." She paused. "But you are now my sworn enemy, Ashlyn, and I will have my vengeance."

"You'll have to have it soon," Noah told her. "Ashlyn's leaving after Christmas."

Jenny smiled with grim satisfaction. "Christmas it is, then."

"Oh, uh… I don't——" Ashlyn glanced uncomfortably at Noah. "I probably won't be here at Christmas."

Emma frowned. "I thought he said you're leaving *after* Christmas?"

"I mean, I am, yeah, but I'm not going to impose again——"

"You have to!" Jenny objected. She looked to Noah. "Tell her she has to be here for Christmas."

"I'm not her keeper, Jen."

"She probably has other plans," Dan put in, with the air of an older cousin who was well-used to refereeing arguments.

Ashlyn had no plans for Christmas, but she'd be damned if she'd admit that pathetic bit of news out loud. So she helped herself to another slug of wine.

"What do you think Aunt Beth did to the potato salad this time?" Aiden asked.

Mercifully, the conversation turned to that disgusting mystery. Ashlyn looked up from her wine glass, catching Aiden's eye and giving him a grateful smile. One corner of his mouth flicked up before he returned his attention to his plate.

"THANK YOU SO MUCH FOR JOINING US!" RENEE WRAPPED her arms around Ashlyn and squeezed tight. She was clearly a little wine-drunk, but the motherly affection was a nice cap to the evening. "You're welcome anytime! Are you sure you had enough to eat? You should take some leftovers. Hang on a minute, I'll put a plate together for you."

"Don't go out of your way," Ashlyn said. "Really, I don't—"

"Nope, nope. You just wait here. I'll be right back."

"Mom, she doesn't—"

"Hush," Renee cut Noah off. "You're getting a plate, too."

Noah and Ashlyn waited docilely while Renee disappeared into the kitchen.

"It's a good thing she never wanted to invade a country or, like, run a bank," Ashlyn observed, amused.

Noah smiled. "She mostly only uses her powers for good."

Renee appeared a few minutes later with two plates piled high with leftovers and wrapped in tinfoil. "Just give the plate to Noah when you're done with it," Renee said. "He'll get it back to me."

"Thank you," Ashlyn told her sincerely. "This is really generous of you. And thank you so much for having me over. I had a great time."

Renee hugged her once more, then hugged Noah. "Alright, kiddos. Drive safe."

Out in the cold, Noah walked alongside Ashlyn until they reached her car, parked along the road in front of the house. The night felt oddly quiet, the silence pressing on her ears like cotton. Overhead, the sky was clear, the moon new, and the stars blisteringly bright. Orion hung directly over the Sorenson house, bold and distinct.

"Thanks for sharing your family with me," Ashlyn told Noah as she reached for her car keys. "See you Monday."

"Ash, wait." Noah's hand landed gently on her arm, stopping her. "How much have you had to drink?"

"Only two glasses. And I finished my last one over an hour ago. I'm safe to drive."

"Okay, good." Then suddenly, Noah's arms were around her, her back was pressed against her car door, and *Noah Sorenson's* lips were on hers. Her plate of leftovers tipped out of her hand, and then she was holding onto him for dear life, opening her mouth to his, savoring the hot, heady taste of him. He kissed like a man who was living his last day—all hungry desperation and uninhibited need. His beard was rough against her cheek, but his lips were soft, his tongue slick against hers. Ashlyn had sworn she wasn't drunk, but kissing Noah made the world tilt and her head spin.

When he finally broke away, their breath mingled as steam between them, rising away in the cold night air. They held each others' gaze for a breathless moment, something chaotic and dangerous and electric swirling in the air around them.

Noah leaned in and pressed one more feather-light kiss to her parted lips. "Now where do I stand in the rankings?" he whispered.

Ashlyn gasped, both appalled and perversely amused that he'd ruin such an intensely heated moment. She pushed against him, claiming space. He backed away, but the smile never left his face.

"You made me drop my plate," she said frostily.

"Here, it's fine. It landed in the snow." He bent to pick it up, handing it back to her, wicked amusement dancing in his eyes the whole time.

"Somebody could've come out and seen that." She snatched the plate from him with prim indignation. "Then there'd be no convincing them I'm not your girlfriend."

Noah shrugged, unconcerned. "See you later, Princess."

He stepped back as she got into her car, then stepped to the side as she pulled away. When she reached the end of the street, she glanced in her rearview mirror. He was still there, a familiar silhouette in the darkness. She hesitated, gripped by the irrational feeling that she shouldn't look away from him or something bad would happen.

But she knew that was silly. And she made herself go.

NOAH WATCHED ASHLYN'S TAILLIGHTS FADE OUT OF SIGHT AS she rounded the corner. He was an idiot to let himself fall for her—*again*. Especially since, this time, he knew she was leaving. In a few weeks, she'd be gone from his life for good. And he'd still be in Lenora, alone, heartsick, and foolish.

nineteen

FRIDAY MORNING, snow fell in swirling wind gusts outside the big picture window in Ruby's Cafe. Inside was glowing and warm, filled with the rich scent of coffee, and the lure of fresh pastries. Ashlyn joined Rose and Laila at a round table near the fireplace. She set her latte and pain au chocolate on the table before settling into the squishy, tufted chair with a satisfied sigh.

"Too bad Dia had to work," she mused, glancing out at the snowy road, hoping her friend's work as a paramedic wasn't in too high of demand with the weather. "I haven't seen her since that night at the Nickel."

"That's the cost of being a contributing member of society," Rose said, blowing on a steaming mug of chai. "How was your Thanksgiving?"

Ashlyn was happy to see her friends. Even though she'd been away for so many years, reconnecting with them felt so impossibly easy, it was like she'd been away for no time at all. Even so, she wasn't ready to hash out what had happened the night before.

"…Good," she answered evasively. "And yours?"

"Hang on." Laila's eyes narrowed. "That was the shiftiest 'good' I've ever heard."

Rose's eyes brightened with interest. "Oh? Tell us more. Family drama?"

"No," Laila said contemplatively. "Her grandma was her only family up here." Suddenly, the suspicious look turned into dismay. "Oh no, were you alone? You should have told me! My parents would've loved to have you over!"

For a second, she was tempted to lie and say she had indeed spent the day alone. But plenty of Noah's family were local, and the community was small enough that someone might blow her lie in a casual conversation.

"No. Renee Sorenson invited me to her place for Thanksgiving."

"Oooh…" Laila was back to sleuth mode. "You spent the day with the Sorensons, and it was… *good?*"

Ashlyn wrinkled her nose. "Don't say it like that. You make it sound lewd."

Laila's brows rose. "Well, *was* it lewd?"

"No!"

"The lady doth protest too much, methinks." Rose smiled slyly. "Go on, Ash. What happened at the Sorensons'?"

"Nothing! I ate a lot of food and played cards with Noah's cousins—"

"Only *Noah's* cousins," Laila said. "Interesting."

Ashlyn frowned. "What's interesting about that?"

"Well, Noah has five other siblings, who presumably have the same cousins, and yet you called them *Noah*'s cousins."

"Well—I mean—" Ashlyn scrambled for an explanation and came up empty.

"Which means Noah is the most significant Sorenson to you. And the way you immediately assumed I was implying something *lewd* makes me think that you and Noah have definitely been up to no good." Laila crossed her arms and leaned back, resting her case.

"Your brain terrifies me," Rose told Laila in an awed tone.

"So, tell us, Ash," Laila prompted. "Did you fuck Noah Sorenson?"

"No! We only kissed," Ashlyn hissed in a defensive whisper.

Rose gasped. Laila looked smug.

"You kissed Noah?" Rose demanded, eyes wide with delighted shock.

"Shhh!" Ashlyn looked around nervously, making sure they weren't overheard.

"But I thought you said Noah hated you?" Rose looked askance.

"That was… a misunderstanding."

"I guess so." Laila picked up her coffee. She tilted her head, a curious smile pulling at her mouth.

A few seconds passed in which nobody said anything, but both friends stared expectantly at Ashlyn.

"I don't have any thrilling news," Ashlyn finally caved under the weight of their stares. "We kissed. The end."

"Hmmm." Laila sipped her coffee.

Rose looked disappointed.

"Anyway, how's the home renovation going?" Laila asked.

Ashlyn shot her a look that said she knew what she was doing but answered anyway. "Good, I think. The new walls are all framed in and drywalled. The new flooring is starting to go in."

"It's going to look totally different," Rose said.

Ashlyn nodded. "That's the plan. I've got all the old wallpaper peeled off, and I'm working on repainting all the rooms."

"By yourself?" Rose asked, surprised.

"Yes," Ashlyn lied firmly. There was no need to bring Noah into this again.

"While you're handling the Winter Market *and* private clients?"

"They don't really add up to all that much work, honestly," Ashlyn said with a shrug. "Ten hours a week, maybe."

"Wait." Laila set her coffee down. "You're taking on private clients? I thought you were leaving in a few weeks."

"I am." Ashlyn's grip tightened on her mug. "I have to."

twenty

NOAH HADN'T TOUCHED her since Thanksgiving, and neither of them brought up the kiss. Instead, he showed up occasionally at her grandma's house to check on his crew, before quickly departing for one of his other worksites. Did he regret kissing her? Probably. Did she regret kissing him back? She probably should.

The problem with avoiding each other was that Ashlyn had finally finished painting all the walls she'd needed to, and now she wanted to tackle the kitchen. But Noah had made her promise to let him help. However, Noah was also currently avoiding her like the plague. She could ask for his help, but that felt a bit like cornering an already scared animal.

So, she swung by Pilkin's Hardware, got herself an assortment of likely tools, and set to doing the work herself. She'd watched dozens of Youtube videos explaining the process of removing all the drawers and cabinet doors, stripping the old paint off, priming and applying the new paint, and replacing the hardware. It seemed a bit tedious, but not overly complicated.

She'd gotten all the lower cabinet doors off and had them laid on tarps in the garage, ready to be coated with paint stripper to remove the hideous primary red paint. She was struggling to fit the screwdriver tip into a painted-over screw when it slipped and skipped across her other hand, opening up a shallow but ragged slash over her knuckles.

"*Motherfucker!*" she gasped, clutching her bleeding hand.

"Ash?" Noah's voice came from behind, startling her.

She whipped around to find him standing in the door-way, looking confused. His gaze dropped to her bloody knuckles and his face fell. He crossed the small kitchen in two strides.

"What'd you do?" he asked, more upset than Ashlyn thought the situation warranted. He grabbed her wrist, tilting her hand so he could see the damage.

"The screwdriver slipped."

"Jesus Christ, I have to take you to the hospital."

"What?" Ashlyn tried to tug her hand back, but Noah wouldn't let go. "What for?"

"A tetanus shot for one thing. Probably stitches, too."

Ashlyn laughed, but his deep frown never wavered. The man was serious.

"Noah," she began placatingly.

"Hey, Sorenson." Anton leaned through the kitchen doorway. "Can you—what's going on here?"

"Nothing," Ashlyn said.

"She sliced her hand open," Noah said, aggrieved. "I'm going to take her to the walk-in clinic."

Anton came closer, peering at Ashlyn's hand, still gripped in Noah's paw. He examined it for a second, then looked up at Noah with a smile. When he registered Noah's utterly serious expression, the smile faltered. "Seriously?" he asked. "You're going to rack up a medical bill for some scraped knuckles?"

"No," Ashlyn said firmly. "I'm *not*. Especially considering I'm out of network up here. It'll end up costing me more than my hand's even worth."

Noah's grip tightened on her wrist. "That's not what you'll say when sepsis sets in."

"Oh my god, Noah, I'm not going to get sepsis. Just let me wash it in the sink."

"Hey, Sorenson," Anton said, calling his attention back. "I got a splinter in my pinkie finger. Will you take me to the hospital, too?"

Ashlyn grinned. "That sounds serious. You probably need an x-ray."

"Alright, fine." Noah released her. "But don't come crying to me when you have to schedule your hand amputation." There was half of a rueful smile in the words. When he met Ashlyn's gaze, something light and warm passed between them.

"Anyway," Anton went on, "I wanted to know if you could send Brick or Langley over sometime this week? The sheetrock's all up and ready to be plastered."

Ashlyn went to the sink and carefully washed the wound with soap and water while Anton and Noah walked off to discuss job details. She was drying her hand with some paper toweling when Noah reappeared beside her with a metal first aid kit. He washed his hands, then popped open the latches, pulling out iodine wipes, antibiotic ointment, gauze squares, and medical tape.

"Noah, it's not a bullet wound."

"Just let me do this," he growled.

She sighed but relented. Noah worked with careful

precision, swabbing the wound with stinging iodine wipes, carefully coating it with antibiotic ointment, then covering it with gauze and taping her up like a boxer about to go into the ring.

"How am I supposed to keep working like this?" She held up her taped hand.

Noah rummaged in the kit again until he found nitrile gloves. He pulled one out and handed to her. "Wear that. It'll keep your bandage clean."

"That's not what I meant. I can barely bend my fingers."

"It's your left hand, you don't even need those fingers."

"Says the man who nearly called an ambulance because he was convinced they were all about to fall off!"

"Uh-oh, Mom and Dad are fighting." Jake grinned from the kitchen doorway.

Noah pinched the bridge of his nose. "What do you want?"

"The flooring nailer needs a new hose—do you have a replacement in your truck?"

Noah scrubbed at his face. "Again? I'm going to throw the whole fucking thing out. Run over to the office and get a different nailer out of storage. Tag this one and throw it in my truck bed."

Jake gave Noah a ridiculous salute and marched off to carry out his orders.

"Tell Anton he can either go with you or take his lunch break!" Noah called after him.

When the front door swung shut, Noah turned back to Ashlyn. "What happened to letting me help?"

Ashlyn shrugged. "Well, you were avoiding me and I wasn't going to wait around for you to decide if you ever wanted to speak to me again."

Something unreadable and minute flickered across his face. He scrubbed at his jaw again, looking up at the ceiling in exasperation. "I was giving you space after I manhandled you. I was waiting for *you* to decide whether we were still good or not."

Ashlyn scoffed. "You barely handled me at all——" Noah looked mildly offended by that, but Ashlyn barreled on "—— and if I wanted space I would've told you so."

Noah regarded her for a silent moment, his gaze intent. "This is the closet all over again, isn't it?"

"No! Because this time, I'm an adult who isn't afraid to spell shit out for you!"

"Spell it out, then."

"I liked the kiss!" She spat the words out almost as an accusation—against who, she really wasn't sure.

A slow smile curled Noah's mouth. He stepped closer to Ashlyn. "Yeah? Am I at the top of the leaderboard, then?"

Ashlyn shrugged. She was so weak for cocky Noah, but she couldn't let him know that. "I mean, you could use a little practice, but nobody's perfect."

His smile sharpened. "If only I had somebody to practice with."

"You're not a bad-looking guy, I'm sure you'll find someone." She slugged him chummily on the shoulder. "Anyways, see you around."

Ashlyn made it two steps before Noah's hand curled around her bicep, reeling her back like a swing dancer. As she crashed against his chest, his lips met hers in a fierce, hot claim. It was just as intense, just as overwhelming, just as *right*, as the Thanksgiving kiss had been. It was better, even. His arms wrapped around her, hauling her up against him as he angled his head to kiss her deeper, sweeter, hotter, needier. She needed more. She needed to feel him. Her uninjured hand found the hem of his shirt and she slipped her fingers beneath it, sliding up his hip until she felt the hot skin along his flank. She curled her fingers into him, feeling sinew and muscle and bone. He groaned against her mouth, leaning harder into her, pushing her back until her shoulders hit the wall.

It's not enough. The thought crossed her mind with an edge of panic. It would never be enough. She needed more of him. She needed all of him. She needed to hold him and taste him. She needed to climb him like a tree. She needed to crush and be crushed by him. She needed to suck his soul out of his body and keep it with her forever and—

She broke away with a gasping breath.

Noah panted raggedly, still holding her close, hands fisted in her shirt, face pressed into her hair. "God damn," he breathed, his voice deep and raw.

They stood locked together, catching their breath, for a long moment. When Ashlyn finally shifted and Noah stepped back, disentangling from each other, the light had changed in the kitchen, and the air was full of electric tension.

"Don't tell me anyone's ever topped that," Noah said, a faint rasp in his voice. He tried to smile and failed.

"No," Ashlyn admitted faintly. "You win."

They regarded one another wordlessly.

"So now what?" Noah finally broke the silence.

"I… don't know."

"You're leaving."

"I know."

"What if—" Noah stopped abruptly, scrubbing at his beard.

"What?" Ashlyn prompted.

"Nothing. Never mind."

"*What?*" she pressed.

He shook his head. "Really, it was nothing." His phone chimed and he plucked it out of his back pocket, glanced at the screen, and cursed quietly. "I have to meet a client. Try not to slice any limbs off while I'm gone? I can help with the counters this weekend."

"Okay."

He started to leave, but almost immediately turned back to Ashlyn. He caught her chin and tipped her face up to press a soft, swift kiss to her lips. "Seriously. Don't hurt yourself. Maybe wait until Jake and Anton get back? That way if you need help, somebody'll be—"

She closed the distance between them and kissed him again, silencing his fretting. "I'll be fine. Seriously." She stepped back. "Go."

He shot her a dubious look, but he gave in and left.

When Ashlyn heard the door shut behind him, she slumped against the kitchen wall and buried her face in her hand.

twenty-one

THE ICON SALON had been remodeled since Ashlyn had last had her hair cut there. The soft, pastel, nineties-era decor that Ashlyn remembered had been replaced by a more modern spa vibe, with lots of potted plants, raw wood, and natural stone tile. The girl at the reception desk smiled as Ashlyn entered and turned to her computer screen.

"Hi, do you have an appointment?"

"Not for my hair. I have a meeting with Linda. Ashlyn Vandale."

"*Oh*, right, Linda's got you on the schedule here." She glanced over her shoulder at the rows of salon chairs. Linda stood behind one, blowdrying a woman's hair. "Linda's just finishing up with a client, and then she'll be right with you. You can have a seat while you wait." She gestured to the small waiting area.

There was already one person in the waiting area, an elderly woman sitting in the middle of all the chairs. Ashlyn gave her a polite smile in greeting as she took one of the end seats, but the woman only stared stonily back at her.

"I heard you were back in town," she said, her aged voice brittle with dislike.

Wonderful. Another Judy Vandale acolyte.

"Do we know each other?" Ashlyn asked flatly, sick and tired of playing nice with her grandmother's memory.

"I should think so!" the old woman said heatedly, fixing Ashlyn with a gimlet eye. "I was only your Catechism teacher for nearly ten years!"

Oh. Janice Albrecht had been the watchful eye that ushered Ashlyn from First Communion to Confirmation. She'd also been her grandma's closest friend. And she was nearly unrecognizable. She'd lost quite a lot of weight. She'd stopped dying her hair. She'd gotten older. Much older. In the time since Ashlyn had left Lenora, Janice Albrecht had gone from merely "older" to downright elderly.

"Mrs. Albrecht, I'm so sorry. I didn't recognize you. It's been a long time since I've been to St. Joseph's."

"It wouldn't have been very long if you'd managed to show up at your grandmother's *funeral*," Mrs. Albrecht said with pointed disdain.

Ashlyn hesitated, uncertain of what to say. Janice Albrecht had known her grandmother as well as anyone could have. No doubt she knew exactly how harsh Judy had been on her granddaughter and found no fault with it.

"Nothing to say for yourself?" the old woman prompted waspishly.

"No," Ashlyn finally said. "I guess not."

Mrs. Albrecht *tsk*ed and turned away from Ashlyn, staring out over the salon with a distant gaze. "To think of everything Judy had to put up with in her life—burying her only son and daughter-in-law, putting up with that husband of hers—"

146

"Her husband?" She had no memories of her grandpa Ronald, but she'd never heard her grandma say anything bad about him, and her grandma *loved* criticizing people. She'd always kept their wedding photo next to grandpa Ron's ashes on the living room fireplace mantel.

Mrs. Albrecht kept going as if Ashlyn had never spoken. "—raising her only grandchild on her own, and all without even the most minimal thanks from that grandchild. No visits. Not even on holidays. Not even at her funeral." She *tsk*ed again. "A shame. An ugly, ugly shame."

"Janice?" A middle-aged woman with a stacked bob and bright red lipstick appeared in the small waiting area. "I'm all set for you."

Ashlyn watched in uncomfortable silence as Mrs. Albrecht shot her one last disquieting frown, then followed the hairdresser over to her chair. Just when she'd started to feel comfortable in Lenora, the universe had reminded her that she didn't belong here. She briefly regretted taking a leave of absence from work and telling so many people she'd be here until after Christmas. Now she was stuck here with more than a month to go.

It's not forever, she told herself. All she had to do was get Grandma's house ready to sell, see the Winter Market through to its conclusion, and then she never had to set foot in Lenora again.

"Ashlyn?"

She looked up, startled.

Linda stood in front of her. "Thanks so much for coming by. How are you?"

"Good," Ashlyn lied, getting up from her seat. "And you?"

"I'm doing alright. Anyways, why don't you follow me into the back—that's where my office is."

Ashlyn forced a polite smile onto her face. "Sure. Lead the way."

EVERY YEAR SINCE STARTING HIS COMPANY, NOAH HELPED put up the Main Street Christmas lights. And every year, he immediately regretted it. And then at some point, in the intervening months, he developed selective amnesia and volunteered to do it for the next one. Well, not this time, he promised himself. *This* time, he would remember that his fingers and face always turned into painful blocks of frozen flesh. He would remember that working with Eric Cole and his thick-skulled sons was like working with three hostile chimpanzees. He would remember that he didn't even decorate his own house for Christmas, so spending multiple freezing cold weeknights decorating a street he didn't even live on was complete madness.

He could've been spending the evening with Ashlyn, putting in the salvaged counters. Instead, he was here, the muscles in his shoulders and neck turning to nothing but knots as he hefted up one massive wreath after another to be affixed to the lamp posts.

And then, as if he'd conjured her through wishful thinking, he spotted Ashlyn coming down the sidewalk.

"Hey, Ash."

"Noah?" She squinted at him.

He had his hat pulled low and a fleece neck warmer pulled up over his face, all the way to the bottom of his eyes. He pulled it down, his breath escaping in a puff of steam. "It's me."

"What're you—" She blinked. "Oh, wait, that's right. The lights."

He nodded, wishing he had more to say. He couldn't think of anything.

"Well, it's looking good so far," she said. "I'll leave you to it."

"Wait."

She paused expectantly.

"Uh… your grandma's house."

She raised her brows, waiting.

"I was thinking—it was built in the late sixties, right?" He latched onto a passing thought he'd had a few days ago.

"Yeah. Sixty-nine."

"Nice."

"Oh my god, grow up." Ashlyn laughed as she spun away from him.

"No—wait! I actually had a point."

She turned back, arms crossed, eyes suspicious.

"The homes in that era often have the lofted ceilings like your grandma's does in the living room."

"Okay…"

"I've seen remodels where they took down the sheetrock and plaster to reveal the wooden trusses. It looks great—like exposed beams. It might be doable in the living room."

"Really?" Ashlyn considered it, skeptical. "It wouldn't just look like unfinished rafters?"

"I did it at my house in the living room and the kitchen. I think it looks good. You could come by and take a look, see what you think."

Ashlyn hesitated, holding his gaze. "Um… sure. I'll take a look."

He realized suddenly that they were both hyper-conscious of the fact that she'd agreed to come over to his house. Neither of them seemed to be able to acknowledge it directly.

"Ashlyn?" Dia Vang stepped out of the drugstore behind Ashlyn. "What're you up—oooh, and *Noah Sorenson*?"

She said it with such knowing amusement, Noah felt a prickle of embarrassment. Did the whole town know he was panting after Ashlyn?

"Dia!" Ashlyn sounded more surprised than pleased, and slightly harried. "I was just going to Ruby's for coffee. Come with me?"

"Sure—whoa, okay." Dia glanced back at Noah as Ashlyn hustled her away. "Bye Noah!"

He watched as they disappeared into Ruby's Cafe. Dia managed to cast him one more speculative glance before Ashlyn tugged her inside the cafe.

"Yo, Sorenson, you planning on handing that cord up one of these days?"

Noah startled back into motion. "Yeah, sorry. Here."

twenty-two

ASHLYN SAT in the high school auditorium half-listening as Carol tried to reason with more of Debbie Schuler's unfeasible proposals. It was the last meeting of the Winter Market committee before the market officially opened for the season, and it was also a public meeting. The rabble were roused, seizing fully on their last chance to air grievances and make absurd demands.

Ashlyn had already made her financial report to the assembly, so her presence at this point was more or less unnecessary. She tried to feel relieved that it was almost over, but mostly she felt a nagging sense of dread. It seemed wrong that she'd be leaving soon. Something felt unfinished, incomplete.

As she ruminated, somebody dropped into the seat next to her. She looked over to see Noah grinning at her, coming in late, as usual.

"Hey, Ash," he whispered.

"You're lucky Debbie's got Carol distracted," Ashlyn whispered back. "Her nerves are about to snap."

He winced. "I actually remembered to set an alarm for this one, but I got held up at a job site."

"Something to add, Noah?" Carol's voice rang out sharply.

"No," Noah said quickly.

Carol fixed him with a beady look before turning back to Debbie. If Ashlyn were in Debbie's shoes, she'd be shutting up and taking cover right about now. But Debbie was not to be cowed. She soldiered on, fervently pleading her case for an opening night parade.

When Carol's attention was wholly on Debbie again, Noah pushed Ashlyn's arm off the armrest between them, shamelessly stealing it.

She stifled a gasp, turning to look at him with silent outrage. He smiled unrepentantly. With pointed deliberateness, she shoved his arm off the armrest and retook it. He casually shoved her off again. When she tried to retaliate, he gripped the armrest as tightly as he could, making his arm immovable. She huffed out an irritated breath and glared at him. He stared straight ahead, pretending to be focused on the discussion happening on stage, but he was grinning like the Cheshire cat.

Summoning her strength, Ashlyn threw her shoulder against his. She must've taken him by surprise because she managed to partially dislodge him. There was a quick scramble to claim the unguarded territory—Ashlyn tried to slide her arm under his, but he caught her and swiped her arm off, but not before she threw her shoulder against his again. He let out a surprised laugh as they grappled.

"*Noah Sorenson*," Carol's voice cut sharply through their amusement. They both froze. "If you have something to say, you should speak up so that the rest of us can hear it."

"No, I apologize, Carol," Noah said in a fair imitation of contrition.

She gave him a look that should have flash-frozen him before turning back to the rest of the assembly.

"Ooooh, you're in *trouble*," Ashlyn crooned under her breath.

"It's your fault."

"It is *not*."

"Because you're bad at sharing."

"That wasn't sharing—that was stealing!"

"Oh, for god's sake," Carol snapped. "Will the two of you either shut up or get out?"

Ashlyn felt her face turn bright red. "Sorry, Carol," she said. "We'll be quiet."

And for the rest of the meeting, Ashlyn did not so much as look at Noah. But she was intently aware of his presence, his nearness. They were both wearing winter coats, but she swore she could feel his body heat radiating against her.

When the meeting was over, Ashlyn walked out side by side with Noah, neither of them speaking. When she reached her car, he leaned against the driver's side door, blocking the handle.

"Come look at the ceiling beams I was telling you about."

"At your house."

"Yes."

She hesitated. She knew she shouldn't. But… "Okay."

Noah's smile returned. "I live out on County R, by the fish hatchery. You know the way?"

Ashlyn nodded.

Noah straightened and stepped away from her car. "See you there."

· · ·

Noah's house was a wood-sided, seventies-era house with a large A-frame entrance, and huge, tall windows over-looking a small lake on the neighboring public land. Pine trees dominated the yard, enveloping the house in green forest, even in December. A stacked stone chimney clambered up one side of the two-story house, and matching flagstones paved the front porch. It was stunningly cozy, but still modern, and somehow distinctly *Noah*.

She followed him inside, her heart in her throat. This was... a decision. Coming here was a choice, and there was no going back.

The entry opened into a long hallway with smooth terrazzo floors and wood-paneled walls. Wood doors lined both sides of the hall. As they strode past them, Noah pointed and explained.

"Bathroom. Basement. Utility room. Upstairs."

Everything was rich, warm earth tones. It could've been drab and dark, but the huge windows and high ceilings made it feel light and bright. The hallway led into a kitchen, which flowed into a dining room with patio doors that opened onto a wooden deck with a pergola. Several bird feeders hung from the pergola, crowded with chickadees, nuthatches, mourning doves, and a beautiful red cardinal male. Further out in the yard, two deer nibbled at the bright green branch tips on a young pine.

"*Deer*," Ashlyn said brightly. She hadn't seen deer casually roaming around since she'd left Lenora. She'd spent the last several years living in dense city centers, where the wildlife mostly consisted of sparrows and pigeons.

"They're always in the yard," Noah said, casting them a brief glance. He turned to the right, stepping through another wide doorway and down into the sunken living room. "Careful," he cautioned. "The step-down is an ankle-breaker if you're not expecting it. I should've raised the floor when I did the renovations, but I liked it too much."

The style of the house all but guaranteed the flooring had originally been carpeting—most likely shag in some unholy shade of avocado green or harvest orange. Noah had replaced it with wide plank wooden floorboards. The A-frame carried through from the front of the house to the living room, with tall sloping ceiling and a triangular back wall filled with floor-to-ceiling windows. The windows over-looked the same view as the dining room. A pot-bellied iron stove sat in the corner, cream-colored brick lining the wall behind it and the floor beneath it. A big stack of firewood sat in a curved iron rack beside the stove. A huge, sage green sectional sofa dominated the space, angled so that both the windows, the fireplace, and the television were in comfort-able view. The wall opposite the windows was covered in built-in shelves, filled with all kinds of books and games and pictures and knick-knacks.

"Watch this." Noah went to the center of the bookcase and reached in to fiddle with something behind a stack of old National Geographics. A *click* sounded, and a portion of the shelving swung forward.

Ashlyn stared, amazed.

"Secret doorway," Noah told her, looking proud of himself.

"But why?" She came forward to examine it. The room beyond was a small space with more built-in shelves, sloping walls, and a desk facing two deep-silled windows. "Is this where you hide your treasure?"

"Nah, I'm just a giant child and I always wanted a secret doorway. This is my home office. To be honest, I hardly ever use it." He shrugged. "Anyways, that's not why you came here. I just don't get to show it off very much."

"You should show it off—it's amazing! *I* want a secret door now."

Back in the living room, he tilted his head up, looking at the ceiling. "See those beams?"

Amber-colored wood beams ran from the peak down to where the A-frame met the short sidewalls. Tongue and groove paneling covered the ceiling, but it'd been left its naturally pale pine color so that it didn't compete visually with the beams.

"Yeah. They look great."

"I'd have to take a look behind the drywall first—your grandma's house is slightly older than mine, so there's a good chance the electrical and the ductwork would make it too big of a job. But if it's not too much work, I think it would change the look of the house entirely. You wouldn't even recognize it."

Ashlyn nodded slowly, imagining it. The idea of making the house completely unrecognizable from the one she grew up in was enormously appealing. "How long would it take?"

Noah looked mildly abashed. "I'd have to come back to it in February. It won't fit into our current schedule."

For a brief moment, Ashlyn considered saying yes. She imagined herself staying in Lenora through the winter. Seeing Rose and Laila and Dia for coffee and girls' nights. Seeing Noah for... anything.

But then reality came crashing down. She knew the sudden leave of absence wasn't reflecting well on her at her firm. If she extended it for two more months, there'd be serious talk about formally removing her from partnership.

That shouldn't feel like a relief.

"I probably should have mentioned that before showing it to you," Noah said.

"It looks great. And, honestly, it'd look great in my grandma's house. But pushing it out to February…"

"Yeah, I get it. It was just a thought."

Silence lapsed. A frisson of *something* passed between them.

"Um…. so…" She needed to leave. Nothing good could come of being alone with Noah. "I should probably head out…"

Noah straightened, his face blanking. "Yeah, of course. I'll walk you out."

twenty-three

NOAH WAITED at the door while Ashlyn stepped back into her boots.

"Sorry you drove all the way out here for nothing," he said.

"No, no, really it's fine. Your house is beautiful. I'm glad I got to see it."

"Thank you."

They were being so excruciatingly polite with each other.

"I wish the timing had worked out because the exposed trusses look amazing. But, you know…" she shrugged. "Can't stay here forever."

"Wh—" He caught himself before the words *Why not?* slipped out of his mouth. "—well," he amended gracelessly, "It's been nice having you here."

Another charged silence fell. Ashlyn was watching him with those inscrutable, deep brown eyes, her expression thoughtful, but otherwise unreadable. Every fiber of his being was attuned towards her, desperate to close the distance between them, to kiss her again.

Her brows drew together, her eyes troubled. "Noah..."

He wasn't sure which one of them moved first. All he knew was that Ashlyn was in his arms, her hot mouth on his, and everything was right and good in the world. She kissed like she was starving for him. She kissed like he was the only thing keeping her alive. The feeling was incredibly mutual. He couldn't think of anything but her, feel anything but her, *want* anything but her.

It wasn't possible for a kiss to feel this good. Ashlyn kept making sexy little sounds, little gasps and moans, that sank beneath his skin and set his blood on fire. Her hands slipped beneath his shirt, stroking over his back, curling into his feverish skin and gripping. He didn't realize he'd backed her against the wall until he felt her hips grinding against his. He was hard and aching for her, and the feel of her body pressing against his cock was more than he could take. He broke the kiss on a ragged breath.

"Wanna see the bedroom?" The words emerged in a hoarse growl.

"*Yes*," Ashlyn said urgently, the tips of her fingernails biting into his skin.

Noah ducked down, scooped Ashlyn onto his shoulder, and straightened. She shrieked as he lifted her, gripping fistfuls of the back of his shirt.

"Noah Sorenson!" she gasped, outraged.

He grinned. She'd forgive him.

"'S'upstairs. Hold on."

"Noah!" Her objection was lost in breathless laughter.

He bounded up the steps with her over his shoulder. At the end of the short hallway, his bedroom door was open and waiting. He strode inside and tossed Ashlyn down on the bed. She glared at him like a wet cat, but it lasted for all of two seconds before she was smiling again. Even without the smile, she couldn't disguise the rapid rise and fall of her breath, the way her fingers curled into the comforter, the way her gaze drifted down his body.

"You could have dropped me," she said, failing to sound properly irritated.

"I lift equipment that weighs more than you on a regular basis." He crawled onto the bed, looming over her.

"I'm Noah Sorenson, I'm so big and strong," she mocked in a deep voice as she pulled his shirt up. He let her pull it over his head. *"I've got big manly muscles and I think I'm sooo*—mmf!"

He crushed his mouth to hers. She yielded immediately to the kiss, wrapping her arms around his neck. When he pulled away she looked flushed and dazed, her lips all swollen and pouting. Only in his wildest dreams had he thought he'd ever see Ashlyn like this. His younger self was having an anxiety attack in the part of his brain where old memories were stored. His present-day self was too enthralled by the woman beneath him to spare a thought for anything else.

"Shirt off," he commanded hoarsely. "I don't want to wreck it." It was a pale blue blouse made of soft, filmy material, buttoned up to her throat by a million tiny, pearly buttons.

Ashlyn reached to her side, confusing him until he realized she was pulling on an invisible zipper.

"Why does it even have buttons?" he demanded, nonplussed.

She laughed, a warm, languid sound. "Because they look nice." She wriggled out of the blouse, back arching, chest thrust out as she pulled it over her head. Noah's mouth went dry at the sight of her perfect little tits, nipples already drawn to tight points.

"Have you been walking around without a bra this whole time?"

She smiled coquettishly. "Yes. I hardly ever wear a bra." She cupped her breasts, plumping them. "Bras are uncomfortable, and it's not like I've got much to fill one anyway."

"Plenty for me." He dropped his head and sucked one pert nipple into his mouth.

"Oh god, Noah!" One of her hands gripped the back of his head as she arched up into his mouth.

He split his attention between both breasts, licking and sucking and nipping until Ashlyn was a writhing, twisting, gasping mess. Having her like this—*making* her like this— was overwhelming in its pleasure. He was drunk on her body, her reactions. His cock was hard and throbbing, his hips convulsively rocking against hers, but he could have spent forever floating in this specific bliss.

"Noah," Ashlyn panted, pushing at his shoulders.

He eased back, mind fuzzy, whole body alive with sensation. Ashlyn pushed herself up, and then she kept coming, shifting her weight forward and pushing him onto his back. She unzipped her jeans and tugged them down her legs with her panties, flinging them onto the floor. Noah started to unfasten his belt, but Ashlyn stopped his hands and took over the task. She eased his zipper down, holding his gaze as she did.

He lifted his hips automatically as she worked his jeans down his hips. His cock sprang free, laying hard and heavy against his abdomen. When Ashlyn had tossed his jeans aside, she bent her head and licked a long, slow stripe along the underside of his cock.

"Jesus!"

It took every ounce of strength he possessed to not thrust upward. His body trembled as her tongue skated over the head of his cock. He tensed, waiting for her to take him into her mouth, but instead, she crawled up the length of his body, and spread her thighs astride his hips. She seated herself with her slick, hot cunt pressing down on his cock.

"Oh, fuck, Ash. Please, honey, don't tease—I'll lose it too early."

She grinned, bracing her hands on his chest, and began a subtle rocking motion, slicking her pussy up and down his shaft.

His hands flew to her hips, gripping like handlebars, holding her still. "It's too much. I don't want to—not yet. Let me inside you, Ash. Please, I need it so bad."

She bent down and pressed a kiss to the center of his chest, where his heart beat thunderously. "Do you have a condom?" she whispered against his skin.

"Nightstand, top drawer." He nodded to the left, then grimaced as her weight shifted over him.

There was the sound of the drawer sliding open, and a moment later, she was sitting on him again. But this time, she positioned her weight on his thighs, leaving his cock exposed.

"Oooh, fresh box," Ashlyn observed, sliding a finger under the flap to break the glue. "Lucky me."

"One of us needs to be."

She smiled as she pulled out a foil and opened it. Taking his cock in hand, she rolled the condom slowly, teasingly down his shaft. She held his gaze while she did it, and her expression as she watched him was as hot and hungry as he felt. He watched in feverish fascination as she straddled him again, positioning his cock at her entrance, and sinking slowly—so slowly—down.

"*Fuuuck,* Ashlyn. Jesus Christ." Her pussy was hot and snug and perfect.

He couldn't take it anymore. He gripped her hips and rolled, flipping her onto her back as he pushed himself deeper into the hot clasp of her body. She gasped, her arms wrapping around his neck and her legs around his hips, pulling him closer.

"Oh, god, Ash. You're taking me so fucking deep."

Noah groaned as he slid in to the hilt, filling her completely. The sensation was just shy of being uncomfortably overfilled, but she welcomed it.

"Who would've guessed my perfect Princess has such an accommodating pussy."

"*Accommodating?*" It was hard to sound disapproving when her voice came out so breathy and soft.

"It's high praise." Her buried his face in her hair as he rolled his hips against hers. "Never want to leave," he panted gruffly, grinding into her with a steady, subtle rhythm. It was a maddening tease—stimulating so many pleasurable nerves, but not hard or fast enough to give her what she truly needed.

She slid her hands down his back to grab fistfuls of his ass. "More, *more*, Noah, give me more," she pleaded impatiently.

"That's my girl," Noah breathed reverently. "So bossy."

"That's not a compliment." She let her nails bite into his ass cheeks.

"Yeah it is." He bent his head and nipped her lower lip. "I've got it bad for brutally honest, demanding princesses."

She laughed. "That's *still* not a—*oooooh*, god, Noah!"

He'd set to fucking her the way she wanted—deeper, harder strokes that filled her all the way up, hitting against that sweet spot deep inside while the base of his cock ground against her clit with each thrust.

Noah had been worried about coming too soon, but Ashlyn was the one who was about to lose it. Each thrust pushed the sensation higher and higher and higher until there was too much to process and it exploded outward in a gasping, arching, twisting crescendo of pleasure.

She was distantly aware of Noah cursing in her ear as her pussy clenched down on him, over and over again, of his thrusts becoming erratic. He clutched her and thrust in deep, powerful tremors running through him, a desperate groan torn from his throat.

When the grip of climax eased, they lay together in panting, sweaty, stillness. Noah's weight was a welcome comfort, like one of those compression vests for dogs who are afraid of thunder. Except Ashlyn was afraid of whatever came next. In the heat of the moment, fucking Noah had been the logical thing to do. Not just logical, but *imperative*. But now the lust fog was dissipating, and Ashlyn was slowly beginning to realize that she'd just made things far more complicated.

Eventually, Noah stirred himself to roll off of her. "One second," he murmured, slipping out of bed to dispose of the condom. When he came back, Ashlyn had pushed herself up to sit, arms wrapped around her bent knees. Noah regarded her almost warily, sitting on the edge of the bed without speaking.

"What now?" Ashlyn asked quietly.

Noah didn't speak right away. She could tell he was picking his words carefully. Finally, he said, "Whatever you want, Ash. I know you're leaving."

God, why did that hurt so bad? He wasn't saying anything she didn't already know. "Right."

"Look, if you want this to be a mistake that we both forget about—" he shrugged "—I can pretend."

"I don't want that," she said quickly. "You're not a mistake, Noah."

He smiled lazily. "Well, then, if you want to keep scratching this itch while you're here…"

She chewed her lip. "I think we can both admit it's going to keep happening. But… I like you, Noah. And I don't want to, you know, catch feelings. Not when I have to leave in a few weeks."

He considered that. "That's fair. What do you suggest, then?"

"We could set some rules."

He raised his brows in question.

"No sleepovers."

"That seems sensible."

"No dates, no being affectionate in public. If other people think we're together, it'll make things messy."

He nodded. "Okay."

"And we both acknowledge that this has an expiration date, and there'll be no hard feelings when I—" she had to clear her throat "—when I leave."

"Of course, Ash." He held out his hand. "Shake on it?"

When she reached out to shake, he grabbed hold of her and pulled her into his arms. He kissed her and she couldn't help but melt into him.

This was a bad idea, but she just didn't care.

twenty-four

THE WINTER MARKET officially opened the Friday after Thanksgiving. It began every year with the official Lighting of the Street—always conducted by a different person or group of people. This year, the official light turners were the high school girls basketball team, who'd won State in the spring. The team stood on the grand stage at the end of Main Street, right in front of the lakeshore, crowded around the switch that would turn the lights on.

Either side of the street was lined with wooden vendors' stalls, trimmed with evergreen boughs and strings of dried oranges and cranberries, shining bells and glittering baubles studding it all. The street was closed to traffic until the market ended and was filled with locals and tourists alike, all heavily swaddled in winter gear. A light snowfall drifted down, settling on hats, hair, eyelashes.

Ashlyn stood in the crowd, face tilted to the unlit decorations strung overhead, listening as everyone counted down in unison.

"...FOUR... THREE... TWO... ONE!"

Up on the stage, the girls slammed their hands down on the switch, and a split-second later, the Christmas lights flashed to brilliant life, filling the street with their festive glow. The crowd cheered and whistled. At the bandstand, a brass band began a jazzy cover of "Sleigh Ride."

"Welcome to the Lenora Winter Market!" the emcee, Tom Meyers, the high school principal, boomed into the microphone. "Thank you all for joining us! Remember to be safe and enjoy yourselves!"

And then there was just pretty snow, Christmas lights, live music, and the sound of a hundred different happy conversations.

As the crowd around Ashlyn thinned, one person remained in place, his gaze fixed on her.

"Noah."

"Hey, Ash."

Her feet carried her over to him without a thought. "I'm going to get some hot cocoa."

"Sounds good."

And that's how they broke rule number two. They spent the entire evening together, wandering from booth to booth, listening to the band, drinking spiked hot chocolate and eating food on sticks, admiring the handmade art and clothing and decor and housewares. Their shoulders brushed as they walked, but he never put his arm around her. He smiled like he wanted to kiss her, but he never leaned in too close. His hand brushed hers now and then, but he never took hold of it.

At some point, they ran into Noah's brother Wes, who joined them. Then they found Lucas and Rowan, the younger Sorenson twins. Then they bumped into Laila and her sister, Daniella, and their little ensemble grew again. But no matter how many people joined them, Ashlyn was wholly, singularly, overwhelmingly aware of Noah. Of his nearness. Of his scent. Of his warmth. Of the memory of his body crushed against hers.

By the time the market closed at ten, Ashlyn was absolutely feral with want.

Alone again, just the two of them, she looked over at Noah, fighting the urge to pounce on him in the street. "I'm going back to the Hideaway," she told him.

He nodded. "That's fine. I don't expect—"

"Because my car's parked there. Then I'm driving over to your place and ripping your clothes off."

A vibrant smile lit up his whole face. "See you there, Princess."

twenty-five

"WOW."

The new flooring was officially all installed. It needed to be stained and sealed, but that would take way less time than installing it had. The new walls and ceiling were all framed, drywalled, and plastered. Now Ashlyn just had to paint them. Combined with the still-in-progress kitchen remodel, the new paint in all the other rooms, and the built-in bookshelf project in the living room that she'd talked Noah into helping her with, the house was almost unrecognizable. It was light, bright, fresh and clean. Gone were the heavy curtains and florid wallpaper. Gone was the hoarder's mess that Ashlyn had struggled to keep up with when she was a child.

"Looks good, right?" Noah asked, sliding a pencil behind his ear.

"It looks… strange." Despite the differences, this was still her grandmother's house, and no matter how many changes she made, Ashlyn still wanted the whole thing out of her hands.

"Good strange?" Noah asked uncertainly.

"Yeah. Of course. Sorry. It's just… it's weird seeing it all cleaned up and nice and…" She shrugged as she trailed off.

"I get it."

Noah stepped closer, and Ashlyn took advantage of the moment to lean against him. He wrapped an arm around her. They stood like that for a quiet moment. Eventually, Ashlyn had to force herself to pull away, or she'd spend all day leaning on him.

"So, I want to finish painting the cabinets before we bring in the counters. Is that okay?"

"Sure. Got a paintbrush for me?"

She'd chosen a soft sage green for the cabinet color, reasoning that green would look good against the golden-brown butcher block counters and the new hardwood floors. The doors and drawer faces were all waiting to be painted in the garage, but Ashlyn was waiting for the slightly warmer temperatures expected the next week.

In unspoken accord, they started on the upper cabinets first—each at one end, painting until they met in the middle. Noah worked methodically, with singular focus. Ashlyn had given some consideration to the idea that they might be too overcome with lust to get anything done, but Noah's focus on his work apparently shut off all the other interests in his brain. They had the cabinets painted in less than an hour.

"We'll let that dry," Noah said as he stood back, taking in their work. "If it needs another coat, we can do that in the morning. Otherwise, we can start putting doors back on."

"Cool. But I'm covered in paint. I think I need to take a shower."

"Okay," Noah said distractedly, still looking over the cabinets for any missed spots or imperfections.

"My only problem is, how will I clean all my hard-to-reach places?"

Noah's head lifted abruptly. Finally, it clicked. A wolfish smile curled his lips. "I suppose I could help you out."

SHOWERS WERE TERRIBLE PLACES TO HAVE SEX. FRUSTRATED, Noah turned off the water, picked Ashlyn's wet body up, and carried her into the bedroom, still dripping wet. He tossed her down on the bed and crawled on top of her.

"That's better," he growled against her ear. "Turn over."

She didn't hesitate, rolling onto her stomach, and wiggling her hips excitedly. "Hurry," she commanded. "God, I need you inside me so bad."

"Bossy," he said, pleased. Ashlyn's plump pussy was on perfect display in the diamond-shaped window formed by her ass and thighs. He was rock hard and aching from thwarted shower sex attempts. He straddled her thighs and positioned the head of his cock against those pillow lips, stroking through her slick folds.

Ashlyn canted her hips up for him, a needy invitation. As he pushed into her, she moaned, back arching as she tilted to take him.

"*Fuck*, Noah, you feel so good," she breathed, hands fisting in the duvet.

He kept her thighs pinned together between his knees as he sank into that plush, wet heat. Ashlyn arched back against him, gasping when he was fully inside her, hips pressed to her ass. He uttered a breathless curse as her inner muscles squeezed his cock. He could stay in that position forever, not moving, just savoring the feeling of being inside Ashlyn.

"Fuck me!" Ashlyn ordered him impatiently, pushing her ass back against him.

"Jesus Christ, Ash, you're so fucking demanding."

"You like it."

He did. With a rueful grin, he adjusted his weight on his hands, and gave the lady what she wanted. He thrust into her with long, hard strokes, pounding until the bedroom was filled with the sound of Noah's grunts, the slap of his hips against her ass, and Ashlyn's gasping cries. She pressed her face to the duvet, ass raised, lost to animalistic pleasure. He'd never expected his straight-laced Princess to be such a fucking tigress in bed. If he'd ever let himself imagine it before, he always thought she'd be sweet and a little shy. This girl, the *real* Ashlyn, was so much better than any of his idle imaginings. It was the only way he knew this was all really happening.

"*Fuck*, Noah, I—I'm going to—" Her words were lost in a helpless cry of pleasure as her pussy clenched down on his cock like a fist.

Somehow, he managed to ride through the obliterating pleasure of her orgasm, though it was a near thing. When her body relaxed against the bed, he bent his head to kiss the back of her neck.

"I want to come on your back," he said impulsively.

She wiggled beneath him. "Do it."

A spike of arousal nearly unmanned him, but he kept control of himself as he pulled out of her and stripped the condom off. One, two, three strokes of his hand, and white-hot pleasure zapped down to the base of his spine and exploded outward. He groaned as he painted Ashlyn's ass and lower back with glistening white stripes. Seeing his mark on her, however temporary, lit up some primal, uncivilized part of his brain, and made him come all the harder.

He collapsed on top of her as the last throes of orgasm left him, smearing his mess between their bodies. Ashlyn let out a little rumbling hum that sounded a lot like purring, wriggling contentedly beneath his weight.

"So much for showering," she said, amused.

"Stay here," he said, grunting as he pushed himself off of her. He went to the bathroom, wetted a washcloth, and returned to the bedroom.

"Ahh," Ashlyn sighed at the sight of the cloth. "A true gentleman."

"We're a dying breed." He cleaned her off, then folded it over and wiped himself off. "Are you hungry?"

"You're going to feed me, too?"

He shrugged. "We said no sleepovers, but there's no rule about cooking."

"That seems like a 'letter of the law, rather than the spirit' kind of thing." She smiled lazily. "But I'm hungry, so yes, please cook for me."

NOAH'S POST-SEX DINNER MENU WAS AMAZING. IT WOULDN'T be served in a five-star restaurant, but it was possibly the most satisfying meal Ashlyn had ever had. He got a bag of dill pickle potato chips out of the pantry and gave them to her. She sat at the island and ate them slowly, watching as Noah put the meal together.

He cooked hamburgers from pre-formed patties in a pan on the stove, and since he didn't have hamburger buns, they ate them on plain white sandwich bread. But he had all kinds of different mustards and relishes and sauces. He talked Ashlyn into putting raspberry jam, hot brown mustard, and garlic mayo on her hamburger, along with pickled jalapeños, blue cheese crumbles, and onion crisps, and it was probably the best thing she'd ever eaten in her life. No restaurant burger would ever compare.

"Oh my god," she groaned, "It's *so* good!"

He smiled, obviously pleased with her reaction.

"If you'd given me enough warning, I could've made buns," she said.

He raised his eyebrows with interest.

"I don't get a lot of time for it, but I really like baking bread. It's relaxing. And it tastes good."

"Homemade buns would've been amazing," he said wistfully.

"These are still pretty damn good." She chomped into hers for emphasis.

As they ate, she looked around the house, admiring it again. For a single guy living alone, he had a remarkably nicely designed and decorated house. It was definitely a guy's house, but in a clean, homey kind of way.

"You don't put up any Christmas decorations?" she asked, thinking how gorgeous a big Christmas tree would look in front of the living room's floor-to-ceiling windows.

He shrugged. "I live alone and don't have many people over. It seems kind of pointless to go through the effort of putting up and taking down decorations just for me."

"I do the same thing in my condo," Ashlyn admitted. "I have this one Christmas wreath I put on my front door so my neighbors don't think I'm a Grinch, but inside… nothing."

"Aw," Noah said pityingly.

"Don't 'aw' me, you're just as sad!"

"Yeah, but I already knew that."

She shook her head, biting back a smile, and turned her

attention back to her burger. "Would you still be attracted to me if I ate three more of these burgers?"

"My attraction would multiply with each one."

Ashlyn laughed. "Noted. Let's see how many I can polish off."

She only managed to eat three-quarters of her second burger. Noah taunted her with the uneaten quarter.

"So close to finishing, and yet you failed." He ate the rest of it in one giant bite. "Your weakness has shamed your ancestors."

"Damn, those bitches are judgy."

Noah cast her an affectionate smile, so warm and sweet it turned her insides to hot syrup. It didn't feel like the kind of smile given to a temporary fuck-buddy. It felt like so much more, and the fact that she wanted it to be more was self-destructive and dangerous.

"I should probably get going," she said as she brought her plate to the dishwasher. "It's getting late, and we said no sleepovers."

Noah mumbled something that sounded like, "*You* said no sleepovers," but he didn't argue with her. He walked her out to her car, kissed the top of her head, and stood on his porch, watching as she pulled out.

God, she was in trouble.

twenty-six

ASHLYN SPENT the next day in the back office of Wagner's Electronics, going over his books and becoming gradually more angry with the service Jeremy had been using. He was right not to trust them. They were sloppy and careless and criminally inept. If Jeremy had blindly trusted their work, he could be facing major trouble with the IRS.

"I'm not a lawyer," she told him, after pointing out the fifth major error. "But I think you have grounds for suing. You already turned in your second quarter filings from them, which are going to have to be amended before the IRS comes after you. They're bad, Jeremy. Like, really bad."

He scrubbed at his jaw, looking fretful. "Can you amend the second quarter filings? I'll pay whatever you want—I can't deal with the IRS right now. We just had our third baby and replaced the roof on our house and..." He shrugged, looking defeated.

"I'll get if fixed. Don't worry."

"Thanks, Ashlyn. You're a lifesaver." And he really, truly meant it. It wasn't the empty platitude delivered by one of the senior partners when she fixed their fuck-up at the firm. Ashlyn's work had literally spared Jeremy and his family a world of grief.

That was a new feeling.

"No problem," she said contentedly. "It's what I do."

After leaving Wagner's, she headed over to her grandma's house to get more painting done. She was finished with the living room and hallway, and wanted to get started on the kitchen walls.

Noah was busy at other job sites, but later in the afternoon he sent her a text telling her to come over to his place after six.

Covered in speckles of paint, Ashlyn went to her motel room to rinse off before hightailing it to Noah's for six on the dot. She shouldn't be so eager to see him. She shouldn't be letting herself get attached. But she just didn't have the will to resist.

When she got to his house, she knocked and let herself in. "I'm here!"

"In the kitchen," Noah shouted back.

She found him pulling a lasagna out of the oven.

"Wow, that smells amazing." She slid onto a stool at the island, watching covetously as Noah set the lasagna pan on a trivet to cool.

"Don't be too impressed, I didn't make it. I got a take-and-bake from Girard's on my way home."

"They've really expanded since I left. Their selling point used to be that they had a little more selection than Larsen's. Now they've got a fancy bottle room and a bakery and a really nice deli."

Noah nodded. "Don't tell my mom, though. She *hates* Stephen Girard."

"Doesn't everybody?" Stephen Girard was rich as

Croesus and wanted everyone to know it. He was flashy and crass and an entitled prick, but he supposedly paid his employees well and provided medical and dental benefits to full-timers. Ashlyn couldn't find the motivation to hate him too much.

"Yeah, but Mom knew him all the way back in kindergarten when he broke all her crayons and put glue in her hair. They have an ancient blood feud."

"Does *he* know they have a blood feud?"

Noah laughed. "Probably not." He turned to the fridge and started rummaging around. "Drink?"

"Diet Dr. Pepper, please."

He fetched one and slid it over to her. "I don't have the stuff to make salad," he said, closing the fridge. "But I did pick up garlic bread."

"That's fine. I had a salad at lunch." She'd had a big Cobb salad at Ruby's, full of colorful vegetables and covered in Ruby's secret dressing.

"Look at you, Miss Healthy."

When the lasagna had cooled enough to cut into, Noah served her a generous portion and then joined her at the island with his own plate. They ate in contented silence. Stephen Girard may have been an asshole, but his deli made an amazing lasagna.

Out of the corner of her eye, Ashlyn became aware of something colorful. She turned her head, looking into the living room—

"You got a tree?" Positioned in front of the big windows, it had to be at least eight feet tall.

"Yeah. Again, don't be too impressed. It's artificial, and it came with the lights and tinsel already on it."

But she *was* impressed. Just last night they'd been talking about how pathetic their Christmas decor was, and now

Noah had gone out and gotten a whole goddam Christmas tree?

"You want to decorate it with me?" he asked.

"You got decorations *too?*"

Noah poked at his lasagna, the back of his neck going slightly red. "Yeah. I mean, I had some already, in a tub from my mom. But it wasn't going to be enough to fill out the tree, so." He shrugged. "They were on sale."

"Noah," Ashlyn said softly, overwhelmed with some foreign emotion. Gratitude, affection, and a weird kind of sadness all mixed in together. It made her want to crawl into Noah's arms and hug him so hard his ribs cracked.

"You like it?"

"Yes, I love it. And yes, I want to decorate it."

"The tree topper's crooked," Noah said, irritated. He went back up the step ladder to fiddle with it.

Ashlyn stood back, an inexplicable knot in her throat as she took in all the lights and sparkling tinsel and glittering ornaments. It was so beautiful, it made her want to cry. And Noah, with his unexpected perfectionism—which Ashlyn found oddly endearing—made her want to cry, too. Happy tears. Which seemed a bit much. So she swallowed hard, and tried to will away the overwhelming sentimentality.

"How's it look now?" he asked.

She'd thought the angel topper had looked straight before, and it still looked straight. "Good," she managed to say evenly.

Noah got off the ladder and stepped back to assess the tree topper, arms crossed. He sighed. "Well. It'll have to do."

Why Ashlyn found his grumpy dissatisfaction with the

glittering angel tree topper so insanely arousing, she would never fucking know. All she did know was that she needed to get his pants off immediately.

"Hm? What are you—" He looked down in confusion as Ashlyn worked his belt open.

"Sit down." She pushed him back, and he went readily enough, sinking down onto the couch. She knelt between his knees and reached for his zipper.

"Ash?"

"I'm so sorry, but I really need to suck your dick."

There was a brief, stupefied silence. Then, "Apology accepted?"

"Oh, good. I was really worried." She tugged his waistband down. Noah lifted his hips, helping her. He was already hard, rigid and thick in her hand. She bent her head, keeping her gaze locked with his, and gently swiped her tongue over the tip of his cock.

He let out a staggered breath. His arms were spread along the couch's backrest, gripping the upholstery with white-knuckled fists.

Satisfied and even more turned on by his reaction, Ashlyn leaned in, bracing herself on his thighs, and took him into her mouth.

"Ah, *fuck*, sweetheart," he groaned, hips flexing minutely. There was a slight tremor in his legs as she worked her way slowly up and down his length.

He was hot and hard and thick on her tongue. She sucked him deeper, trying to relax her throat, trying to take all of him. Noah made a strangled noise, his whole body quivering and tense. Doing this to him, making him weak like this, was so arousing, she thought she would combust. She could feel her own wetness when she shifted her body, sensitive folds slick against each other, soaking the gusset of her panties.

She teased herself by teasing him, drawing the pleasure out, bringing him close, but never completely over the edge. She worked him into a groaning, cursing, trembling wreck, until he couldn't take it anymore. He let go of the couch cushions and slid his fingers into her hair, gripping it in a desperate fist.

"Ash, you're going to fucking kill me. Let me come, sweetheart."

The commanding fistful of her hair combined with the pleading endearment made her arousal skyrocket. If he tugged a little harder and said "pretty please," she might just come on the spot. She took him hard and deep, his shaft gliding over her tongue in swift, plunging strokes. She sucked on him, pulling him even deeper, where the flexing movement of her throat muscles wrapped around his cock head, and finally brought him over the edge.

He gasped her name hoarsely, fist tightening in her hair, keeping his cock buried as he came in hot pulses down her throat. "Fuck, fuck, *fuck*, Ashlyn. *Ashlyn.* Jesus Christ." He let out a haggard breath as he released her. She barely managed to wipe her lips before Noah pulled her up onto the couch with him and took her mouth in a deep, fierce kiss. He must have tasted himself on her, but he didn't seem to care. He let his weight fall over her, pushing her back. When she was sprawled beneath him on the couch cushions, he drew back and reached for the button on her jeans.

Ashlyn squirmed as he worked her jeans and panties down her legs. Legs freed, he grabbed her ankle and lifted it until he could set her heel on top of the couch's backrest, spreading her wide for his perusal. She was too needy to be embarrassed. The room was lit only by the soft, multicolor glow of the tree lights, and Noah was staring at her like she was Christmas dinner.

Holding her gaze with that hungry glint in his eye, he sank down, bringing his mouth to her hot, wet core. His tongue swept along her pussy, from entrance to clit. When he found that sensitive little crest, he stroked over it again and again.

It was too good, too much. Ashlyn's thighs tried to close, but Noah gripped them with his big, rough hands, keeping her spread wide as he feasted on her. Ashlyn writhed, hands thrown over her head, back arching. She was already so close, and he was right on her clit, strumming her higher and higher. He closed his lips around it and gently sucked, and she was gone. Her back bowed off the couch entirely, her legs shaking, throat raw as she cried out with each crashing wave of pleasure.

As the climax receded, Noah was still gripping her thighs, pressing gentle kisses along the inside of one.

When he saw that she'd come back to herself, he eased her leg back down. "I forgot to tell you—I picked up ice cream, too. Do you want some?"

Ashlyn stared at him. She was perilously close to offering to bear his children. "What kind of ice cream?" she managed to ask in a sane-sounding voice.

"Moose Tracks."

"Oh, god, yes."

He hoisted his jeans back up as he stood, zipping the fly and refastening his belt. "Stay here, I'll bring you a bowl."

She watched him go with a dazed sort of wonder. After a few seconds, she remembered her ass was bare and went looking for her pants and underwear.

When Noah came back, she was sitting cross-legged on

the couch, admiring the tree. He handed her a generously filled bowl of ice cream and sat down next to her.

"You know what I always do on Christmas?" she mused, eyes fixed on a Rudolf the Red-Nosed Reindeer ornament.

"Hm?"

"Remember those old claymation Christmas movies? The ones from, like, the sixties?"

"Yeah. I always liked those."

"I watch those on Christmas every year. Usually by myself."

Noah glanced at her. "Wanna watch one now?"

"Really?"

"Yeah. I bet we could stream one."

She crossed her legs and settled more comfortably on the couch. "Okay. Rudolph's my favorite, if you can find it."

He smiled. "Alright, let's see." A few minutes later, he'd found Rudolph the Red-Nosed Reindeer, and had it playing. Ashlyn scooched closer, leaning against him as Burl Ives's voice emanated soothingly from the speakers.

MUCH LATER, NOAH AWOKE IN THE CHRISTMAS TREE'S SOFT glow. The TV screen was dark. He was stretched out on the couch, a blanket laid over him, and Ashlyn lay spooned against him. He had no idea what time it was, but he also didn't care. He'd never been so comfortable in his life. He pressed a kiss to the top of Ashlyn's head, then laid his head back down and closed his eyes.

That's how they broke rule number one.

twenty-seven

WHEN ASHLYN WOKE, she was immediately aware that she wasn't in her bed at the Hideaway. She was stretched out on Noah's couch—an insanely comfortable couch—with Noah's warm bulk spooning against her from behind. She knew exactly how it had happened.

It'd started because she'd been a little cold and wanted a blanket, which Noah fetched for her. Then she'd wanted to be more comfortable while they watched the second movie, so they both agreed to stretch out. Then, when she'd felt her eyelids getting heavy, instead of telling Noah that she needed to leave, she'd simply burrowed against him and drifted off. Intentionally! Like a self-destructive, overly-attached fool!

Noah was probably going to be weird about it. They'd explicitly agreed to no sleepovers, and here she was, a flagrant rule violator. Maybe she could sneak out? Noah seemed like a heavy sleeper. Moving carefully, she disentangled herself from his embrace and slipped out from under the blanket. She stood over him for a second, making certain he hadn't woken. And also, if she was being honest with herself, taking the opportunity just to look at him.

She was still in the middle of being a besotted creep when a sudden, blaring alarm nearly sent her through the roof.

Noah cracked one eye open lazily, and reached behind himself, pulling his phone out of his back pocket. He silenced the ear-splitting alarm and looked up at Ashlyn. A sleepy smile spread over his face. "Good morning."

Ashlyn's heart was still racing from the jump scare of his alarm. "How are you just laying there after an air raid siren went off in your back pocket?"

He yawned and pushed himself up to sit. "I'm a heavy sleeper. I need a loud alarm." He rubbed at his face and scratched his fingertips through his beard. "Want some breakfast?"

She was a little surprised by his nonchalance, but she decided to roll with it. No sense in making a bigger deal out of it than it needed to be. "Sure. Do you have coffee?"

"I might have some instant stuff in the cupboard. I usually grab a coffee at Ruby's on my way into town, and then refill from the pot at work."

"Oh, then I'll just swing through Ruby's, too."

Noah got up from the couch and went into the kitchen. Ashlyn followed.

"I wish I had time to offer something better, but I've got to be at a job site in about an hour. How's an egg sandwich sound?"

"You don't have to—"

"I'm already making myself one. Doesn't take any more time to put two more eggs in the pan."

"Oh, well... alright. Sure. Thank you."

"Yolks runny or cooked?"

185

"Runny."

In short order, Noah had toast in the toaster, and four eggs sizzling away in a frying pan on the stove. He sat beside her at the island when they were done, and they ate in comfortable silence. Another alarm went off on his phone, this one at a much more tolerable volume.

"Oh, shit." He got up, going to one of the cabinets above the sink.

"What's wrong?"

"Forgot my meds." He pulled a transparent orange prescription bottle out and shook a single tablet into his hand.

"Is that what the alarm was for?"

"Yeah." He swallowed the pill dry, then bent his head to drink from the sink tap. "I've got alarms for everything. Wake up. Take your meds. Leave for work."

"Pick up Ashlyn at the Hideaway."

He grimaced. "Ash, I'm really sorry about that, I—"

"Shhh. I was teasing. Come finish your sandwich."

He slid back onto his stool and resumed eating. When they were both done, Ashlyn cleared his plate with hers and loaded them into the dishwasher. "Thank you for breakfast," she said.

"Any time."

"Alright, well, you've got to be at work, and I've got a meeting with Carol this morning, and I need to shower and change clothes, so I'm going to head out."

"See you later at your grandma's place."

"Thanks, Noah. I—" She wanted to say so much more than she should. Swallowing the words, she gave him an uneven smile. "I had a lot of fun last night. I'll see you later."

And then she ducked out before she said anything too emotional.

At Ruby's, Ashlyn had just stepped inside and joined the line to order when the door jingled again behind her and a familiar voice said, "Well, fancy seeing you here."

She turned, unable to stop the brilliant smile spreading across her face. "Noah!"

"You look good," he told her. "I like seeing the two sides of you. Rumpled-up morning Ash, and then polished, professional Ash."

"Noah," she warned in a low voice, gaze darting around to see if they were overheard.

He lowered his voice too, his smile turning devious. "Makes me want to rumple you up again."

"*Noah Sorenson*," she hissed through a silly smile. "Behave yourself."

He straightened with an air of reform, but the knowing smirk never left his face. "I don't think I—"

"Ashlyn?" Rose Reznik's voice came from the direction of the counter.

She turned and saw Rose waiting for her order to be made. "Oh—Rose! Hey!" She knew her voice was a little too loud, a little too bright, and that a telling heat was creeping over her face.

Rose's attention shifted slightly behind Ashlyn. "Oh, Noah?" She paused, a calculating look on her face. It slowly turned into a victorious one. "Are you guys here together?" she demanded, excited. "Laila was right!"

"No she wasn't," Ashlyn said quickly.

"*Hmm*," was all Rose said.

"Double-shot vanilla latte for Rose," one of the baristas called.

"That's me." Rose turned to get her drink, then hurried over to Ashlyn and Noah. "You're lucky I have to get to work because I have *so* many questions, woman."

"There's nothing to talk about," Ashlyn lied badly.

"Sure," Rose agreed with an eye roll. "Welp, got to go. Nice seeing you, Noah!"

"See you, Rose."

And then she was gone and the silence between Noah and Ashlyn was instantly awkward and tense.

"She's definitely going to tell Laila and Dia that she saw us together," Ashlyn finally said. "But I don't think we have to worry about them spreading it around town. They're not gossips. Well, not outside of themselves."

"So the secret's safe." He sounded oddly bitter as he said it.

Ashlyn glanced at him, but his face was impassive. "Noah—"

"Good morning! What can I get for you?"

Ashlyn swallowed whatever words had been about to come out of her and turned to face the barista. "Morning, Ellie. Just a medium coffee for me."

NOAH WAS IN A GRAY MOOD FOR THE REST OF THE MORNING. He didn't know why Ashlyn's reassurances of secrecy were so annoying to him. That's what they agreed on, wasn't it? But as he dwelled obsessively on it, he realized that he might have subconsciously believed that if other people found out about the two of them, it would... change things? How and why they would change wasn't exactly clear to him, but clearly he'd expected Rose's discovery to lead to something bigger than just "don't worry, you're still a secret."

Maybe it was the secret thing that was rubbing him wrong. He knew why they'd decided to keep things discreet. If word got out, Noah's the one who'd have to live with the fallout. Ashlyn was leaving, so really, she was doing him a favor.

That didn't stop it from feeling like an insult.

When he finished the assessments at the Pleasant Pines apartment complex, he drove over to Ashlyn's grandma's place. He didn't really have any reason to be there, except he knew Ashlyn would be there.

When he pulled up, Ashlyn's car was parked out front, and the overhead garage door was raised about two feet.

Confused, he parked behind Jake's truck in the driveway, and walked over to the garage door. He crouched and peered beneath it.

Ashlyn was inside, crouched over a tarp littered with cabinet doors and drawer faces. He watched for a few seconds while she used a paint roller to apply sage green paint to one of the cabinet doors.

"Hey," he said.

Ashlyn jumped about a foot, looking around in startled bewilderment. "Noah?"

He bit back a laugh. "Over here. Under the garage door."

She squinted in his direction. "It's so bright out there, I can hardly see you. Come inside."

He let himself in through the security door. "Got the garage door lifted for ventilation?

She nodded, still painting.

"Smart. But, just so you know, paint can freeze. You should run a space heater out here while the paint's drying."

189

She cocked a finger gun at him. "That's why I keep you around. For your big brain."

He pretended at confusion. "I thought it was for my big—"

"Oh my god, don't say it," she groaned.

"—heart."

She shook her head. "Lame recovery."

"You won't think I'm so lame when I tell you I have two space heaters in my truck."

"Ooh, no, you're the coolest. You and your big... heart."

He wanted so badly to haul her into her arms and kiss her senseless, and then maybe bend her over the workbench in the back corner of the garage, but Jake and Anton were both inside, staining the new flooring, and could potentially come out to the garage at any time.

So he settled for clearing his throat awkwardly and leaving to get the space heaters. When he got back, he helped Ashlyn finish painting.

"When they're not tacky to the touch, we should take them inside. They'll need to finish drying overnight, and it's not safe to leave the space heaters running that long."

"Ugh," Ashlyn groaned, dismayed by the extra work. "Fine. You're the expert."

LATER, AFTER JAKE AND ANTON HAD GONE HOME FOR THE day, they moved to the living room to begin working on the built-in bookshelves Ashlyn wanted on either side of the fireplace. Noah would've helped her build an ark in the living room if it gave him an excuse to spend more time with her.

"Alright, so you're going to drill right there, right through the jig."

She followed his directions, drilling tidily into the pine board.

"Good girl, that's it," he said encouragingly.

Her gaze flashed up to his, gleaming with dark intensity. A small, wicked smile curled the corner of her mouth, sending a hot flash of lust straight through his core.

She set the drill down. "If you're looking for a good girl, I'm afraid you've come to the wrong house."

"I'm—*oof*—" He started to apologize but his words were abruptly cut off when she shoved him up against the wall. She was several inches shorter than him and had to be at least thirty pounds lighter, but she'd pulled some kind of using-his-mass-against-him type of esoteric martial arts move, and now he was staring wide-eyed at her, both alarmed and undeniably aroused. Her fists were curled in his work shirt, her forearms pressed to his torso. The rest of her body was so close to his, he swore he could feel the electromagnetic charge of her skin buzzing against him.

"—sorry?" he finally managed to finish his sentence after an unsteady breath.

Her grin turned roguish. "Bend down so I can kiss you."

"What?" The word tumbled vaguely out of his mouth, even as his body automatically complied, bending down to her level.

"Now who's a good girl?"

Before he could be affronted, her lips were on his. The kiss turned hot and heavy, and Ashlyn's hands slid down his torso to find his belt buckle.

"I don't have a condom," Noah groaned against her lips.

She sighed, hands going still. She glanced at the

sawhorses and the stack of boards that needed guide holes drilled into them.

She looked back at him. "Call it an early night?"

"Meet me at mine?"

She cast him a feral little smile. "If you don't have a condom ready when I get there, I'll just use your face."

Noah stiffened. "Fuck, Ash, *yes*, do that."

HE GOT INSIDE JUST AS ASHLYN PULLED IN. SHE MET HIM AT the door and they crashed together like waves. The kiss was frantic, their hands rough. They fumbled blindly for the stairs, undressing each other clumsily as they went.

In the bedroom, Noah let Ashlyn shove him onto the bed. He beckoned her towards him, and when she clambered over him with her lithe, naked body, he hooked his hands beneath her thighs and dragged her forward.

"Bring that pussy here," he growled.

She made a sound that was half laugh, half gasp, and did as he ordered, crawling forward to kneel on either side of his head. She spread her thighs, bringing that hot, sweet cunt to his mouth. He licked and sucked at her slick flesh, hands gripping her thighs, cock throbbing with each desperate little gasp she made. When she came, her whole body shook, each breath escaping as a keening cry. When it eased, she slid off of him, breathless and dazed.

"Grip the headboard," he said.

She moved to obey while he put the condom on. When he came up behind her and grasped her hips, she shivered, bowing her head. He positioned himself against her and pushed in with one hard, deep plunge.

"*Ah!* Noah!" she cried, hips canting up to take him all the way. "God, you feel *so* good. So, *so* good."

Spurred by her words, he fucked her hard and fast, a desperate hunger driving him like a madman. Ashlyn rocked back against each thrust, their bodies slapping together as the bed creaked beneath them. Noah's breath rasped in his throat, an in-and-out saw that matched the feverish pace of his thrusts. Ashlyn suddenly cried out, back arching, as her pussy squeezed around him, milking him, dragging him into orgasm with her. Their voices tangled together like their bodies, shared exclamations that only made sense together.

When at last the frenzy released them, they lay slumped crosswise on the bed, Noah on his back, Ashlyn splayed across him.

"Damn, Princess," he breathed. "You know how to fuck."

"It helps to have a top-notch competitor in the ring with you."

Noah laughed breathlessly. "Are you finally admitting I took gold?"

Ashlyn laughed with him. "Am I an Olympic event now? I'm going to get an ego."

"You're an event, alright." He shifted his weight, rolling so that he was on his side and Ashlyn was in his arms. He kissed her, playfully rough at first, but then, without really meaning to, gentling into something tender and slow.

He was in deep fucking trouble.

"I can't believe you're single," Ashlyn said when they'd been lying sleepily together for a few minutes.

He'd had this conversation on a regular basis with all his older relatives, but it didn't make him cringe when Ashlyn brought it up. It made him contemplative.

"I spent the first half of my twenties screwing around. Then when I started getting my life together, I didn't feel like it was fair to anyone else to try to have a relationship. Then, once things started coming together for me, I'd gotten in the habit of being alone. I'm not even entirely sure I know how to be in a relationship."

"You're doing pretty good with me," Ashlyn said. A split second later, she stiffened in his arms. "I mean, not that we —you know, it's not, like, a *real* relationship, but… it's good. I like being with you."

"I like being with you, too," Noah said, too pleased by her slip of the tongue to want to save her from her own awkwardness. "So how come you're still single? Gorgeous, smart, funny, fucks like a cat in heat? You're the whole package."

"Are you telling me that *I* took gold?"

"Gold, Silver, and Bronze. No one else even made it on the podium compared to you."

She obviously hadn't expected sincere agreement. "Oh. Well. Noah, that's… you've got all the medals, too. For me."

He lifted his head to see if she was blushing. She was. He smiled and laid his head back down. "So why are you still single, then?"

She sighed. "I don't know. I've dated. I've had boyfriends. But none of them ever worked out, for whatever reason. I think I'm too bossy."

"You're the right amount of bossy."

"I can be kind of sarcastic, which men don't seem to like."

"I like it."

"I'm kind of closed off."

"I don't think so."

"Maybe I'm not as closed off with you," she said hesitantly.

"So you're telling me everyone you dated broke up with you because you're bossy, sarcastic, and closed off?"

"Well, not in those words. And to be fair, I'm not constantly getting dumped. At least half the time, I was the one calling it quits."

"Why?"

She shrugged. "I just want to feel like I'm someone's first choice. I've *never* had that feeling. But I see it with other people, and I want it so bad. I want to be someone's priority. And with most of the guys I dated, I felt like I just kind of fit neatly into their life and that's why they wanted to be with me. Not because I was anything special, but because I was convenient."

He wanted to tell Ashlyn that she was more than special to him, that she would easily be his priority if they were really together, but he knew that would be saying too much, so he kept it in.

"I'm sorry, Princess." He kissed the tip of her ear. "I don't think I really know that feeling either. I'm always the supporting actor in other people's lives."

"That's it exactly." Ashlyn twisted in his arms to face him. "I want more than that."

I could give you more. He didn't say it. He couldn't. Because he could give her his whole heart and make her his first choice always, but she had a high-flying career back in Chicago, and he'd be an ass if he asked her to give all that up because he laid good pipe and sometimes brought lasagna home from the grocery store.

Speaking of…

He lifted his head. "Hungry?"

She stretched lazily. "Kind of. Got any ice cream left?"

195

twenty-eight

DAYS PASSED IN FRAUGHT HAPPINESS—
WORKING together when Noah's schedule allowed,
meeting at his house after work to get each other off, and
then hanging out together and knowing it all had an expiration date. Ashlyn brought groceries and made them both
dinner several times instead of relying on him to cook every
night. She was careful not to spend the night again, but that
did nothing to stem the growing intimacy between them.

And then, one day, with only a week until Christmas,
they were done with the house, and with it, Ashlyn's reason
for remaining in Lenora.

"So the guys finished getting the trim up this morning,"
Noah told her as he walked through the remodeled house
with her. "What do you think?"

The floor looked beautiful and uniform throughout the
house. The walls were clean and freshly painted. The
kitchen was airy and bright. The living room was inviting
and spacious. She stared at it all, knowing she should be
elated by the change, but unable to be truly pleased with it.

"It looks amazing," she said truthfully. "I can't believe what a great job you guys did."

"You did a ton of work, too," Noah pointed out. "The kitchen's basically all you."

She smiled faintly. She was proud of all the work she'd put in, but when she looked at the kitchen, she didn't feel any of the pride. She just felt a deflated sense of regret.

"I can't believe it's all done." She looked around, weirdly hoping to find some overlooked bit that needed fixing. "I guess I better find a real estate agent."

Noah nodded. "Might be good to put it on the market while there's so much traffic in town for the market. You'll get more people to come take a look at it."

"Yeah," she agreed distractedly. "Good idea."

"Well, look, this was a big job. I know your relationship with your grandma made it difficult, but you got it done. Come to my place and we'll celebrate."

She smiled. "Oh yeah? How're we going to do that?"

"I was thinking of throwing a tasteful orgy."

"Noah!"

"Alright, just the two of us, then."

She shook her head, grim mood dissipating in the face of Noah's irrepressible charm. "I'll be right over."

He dropped a kiss on the top of her head as he walked to the front door. "Sounds good. See you in a bit."

NOAH'S CELEBRATION WAS A FANCY LITTLE CHOCOLATE CAKE from Girard's bakery and pizza from Luigi's. The fact that he must've bought the cake and ordered the pizza ahead of time, already planning a celebration for her, twisted her heart like an old rag. Part of her was wounded that he wanted to celebrate the end of her reason for being in

Lenora. But another part of her was so touched that he wanted to celebrate this big milestone with her.

Fully aware that that was a really contradictory set of feelings, but too muddled to sort them out, Ashlyn pushed tiresome thoughts and feelings away, and let herself fall entirely into the physical. She all but pounced on Noah as soon as he set the pizza box on the counter, kissing him like she needed the oxygen from his lungs.

He went along readily with her ferocity, giving as good as he got, throwing her over his shoulder and taking her to his bed like a caveman. She wrestled with him, refusing to be pinned down, but also egging him on to try. Noah was strong, but Ashlyn knew she could be a slippery eel. When he finally got her pinned, they were both panting raggedly, bodies sheened with sweat.

He crouched over her, wrists trapped above her head, his gaze intent upon her. Ashlyn waited for his next move, anticipating more roughness. Instead, he bent his head and kissed her gently, tenderly, sweetly, until her tense, agitated body relaxed against his. Until she returned his kiss with equal tenderness, equal need. They undressed each other with playful patience. When they finally fitted their bodies together, Noah sank in with gentle care, stretching her so slowly that she felt every individual millimeter of penetration.

She gasped his name as they moved together, a sweet, slow dance that brought her to the edge and kept her there for what seemed like forever. And when she finally tipped over, Noah was there with her, breathing her name like a prayer as his body shuddered over her, around her, in her. She felt him everywhere. Her skin, her muscles, her bones, her soul. Noah had worked himself deep, and Ashlyn didn't think she would ever fully escape him.

"You okay?" he asked as they lay together in the dark.

"Yeah," she lied. "You?"

He was quiet for a moment. "It's okay if you're not okay, Ash."

She hugged her arms tightly around him, burying her face in his chest. "I'm just having an emotional breakdown over my grandma's house. It's... weird. I just... I don't know. I don't know how to feel about it."

He pulled her tightly against him. "I get it. It's a big deal. If you want to talk about it, I'm always here."

Ashlyn nodded silent acceptance. Noah's lips brushed the top of her head.

Ashlyn stood with Debbie Schuler—Winter Market provocateur and premier real estate agent—in the front hall of her grandma's house. She glanced at the time on her phone for the fifth time.

"Relax," Debbie told her, idly smoothing her blouse. "Nobody charges through the door at the exact moment an open house begins."

"I know," Ashlyn said, sounding anything but relaxed. "I just... it's weird. Selling this place. It—" *It never felt like mine* wasn't something you say to your real estate agent. She wished Noah were here. He'd understand. He'd help her calm down.

"You grew up here," Debbie finished for her, nodding sagely. "I understand. Selling your childhood home is an emotional process."

"Yeah," Ashlyn agreed vaguely. "It definitely is."

Footsteps sounded on the front walk and Ashlyn stiffened. Debbie hurried to the front door, pulling it open to greet the potential homebuyers. Ashlyn's stomach churned as she watched a smiling young couple with a toddler step inside.

Debbie chattered pleasantly with them, introducing Ashlyn before sweeping into the living room. Ashlyn remained in the hallway, listening distantly as Debbie extolled the house's virtues, oddly conscious of her own heartbeat.

The door opened again, and Ashlyn stepped back, not certain how she was supposed to greet even more people.

But it wasn't a stranger coming in—it was Mrs. Albrecht. Ashlyn's stomach turned to lead. She immediately started sweating. She felt like she was in trouble. Like she'd been *caught*. But caught doing what?

Nothing, she reassured herself. *You haven't done anything wrong. You're not in trouble.*

"Ashlyn," the old woman greeted her with cold reserve.

"Hi Mrs. Albrecht," she managed to respond, even if her voice came out hoarse.

As her gaze lifted from Ashlyn to the hallway, her stony expression dropped into one of complete surprise. "Oh my — oh! It's so different!"

Ashlyn swallowed, trying to get ahold of herself. "Yeah. We had to repair some damage, and then since the house was already being worked on, I figured I'd do some small renovations."

"It's not just that. It's the—well, the garbage. All the stuff Judy couldn't let herself get rid of. It's gone!" She strode down the hallway, peering into the living room, the den, the kitchen.

"You knew about the hoarding?" Ashlyn asked, trailing after her in shock. Grandma had *never* bared her flaws or weaknesses with *anyone*.

Mrs. Albrecht sighed, smoothing her hand over the new kitchen counters. "Yes, though I don't suppose I saw the worst of it. I tried to help her sort through things, get stuff thrown out, but it was impossible to keep up with. After a while, she stopped letting me in the house."

That sounded more like the grandma Ashlyn knew.

"I know why," Mrs. Albrecht went on. "Judy needed to be in control. She needed to be perfect. Being capable and competent was always of the utmost importance to her."

Yep. That was definitely the grandma Ashlyn knew.

Mrs. Albrecht shook her head. "Ron's been gone thirty-five years, and Judy spent every one of them still demonized by that man."

Ron was her grandfather's name.

"He—what? My grandpa?"

Mrs. Albrecht glanced at her, back to her icy composure. This was no special bonding moment—Mrs. Albrecht was about to tell her something that would hurt. "Ronald Vandale was a cruel, vicious, snake of a man. Judy had to have everything perfect all the time, or he'd come down on her like a pile of bricks. Screaming, cursing, making her life miserable."

Was that the source of it all? Was that why she'd become an obsessive and controlling perfectionist who constantly held Ashlyn to impossible standards, and then punished her as the worst criminal when she failed to meet them? Was it some sort of defense mechanism? If Grandma could make Ashlyn perfect, then Ashlyn would be safe? It was a generous interpretation, and Ashlyn wasn't in the mood to be generous.

Mrs. Albrecht straightened her spine suddenly, seeming to steel herself for a confession. "I was glad when he died."

"Yeah, I can imagine."

Mrs. Albrecht did a double-take. She clearly wasn't expecting that response. It took her a second to find her composure, to find words. "You— Don't you…" She shook her head, looking away from Ashlyn to gaze around the renovated house. "Well, then. I suppose I've finally said my piece, after all these years."

"You never told Grandma?"

"No," Mrs. Albrecht said with strong feeling. "I didn't dare. Any time I criticized Ron, Judy would get horribly upset. Anxious. Looking over her shoulder, wringing her hands. I couldn't do it to her. But I lit a candle every Sunday for years, praying that God would grant His mercy to Judy, and then Ron Vandale up and dropped dead of an aneurysm. So miracles do happen."

Ashlyn blinked. She wasn't sure how to reconcile this openly vengeful woman with the strictly self-righteous woman who'd taught her CCD classes for so many years.

Mrs. Albrecht seemed to have shocked herself as well. She smoothed her hair and straightened her already-straight collar. "Well. It's a shame that it happened under these circumstances, but it's a relief to see the house clean and in good repair. I know Judy doesn't need it now, but still…"

"It was kind of therapeutic getting it all fixed up," Ashlyn admitted.

For a brief moment, Mrs. Albrecht's flinty gaze softened. But just as quickly, it was gone again. "Well, I doubt we'll cross paths again. So, goodbye, Ashlyn."

"Goodbye Mrs. Albrecht."

Ashlyn watched from the kitchen as the crotchety old woman saw herself out.

A second later, Debbie appeared, looking mildly confused. "Who was that? A buyer? Did you give her my card?"

Ashlyn continued to stare down the empty hall. "No, she wasn't looking to buy."

By the time the open house finished, they'd had a few more people come in. Ashlyn couldn't remember a thing about any of them. As she locked the house up, Debbie pulled the OPEN HOUSE sign out of the yard.

"This was a good showing," Debbie told her confidently.

"Yeah?" It didn't feel good.

"I think that first couple will make an offer."

"Oh, um… good?"

"Well, we'll see what the offer is." Debbie threw her things into the back seat of her car and walked around to the driver's side. "Anyways, if we don't get any respectable offers, why don't we plan another open house for two weeks from now?"

"Sure."

"Alright, well, I'll be in touch. Have a nice night."

As Debbie drove away, Ashlyn stood on the front walk, staring up at the house that used to be her prison, feeling melancholy and strange. She was done. She'd repaired the house, remodeled it, and now she was selling it. She should feel relieved that she was about to leave it behind forever, but all she felt was vague resentment that she was being pushed out by a ghost.

The cold finally became too much, and, shivering, Ashlyn got into her car. She started the short drive to the Hideaway, but only a block away, she turned back around and headed out of town, towards County R.

· · ·

Noah answered the door with a smile that immediately shifted into an expression of concern. "Is everything okay?" he asked, ushering her inside.

"It should be," she said tiredly as she kicked her boots off and slipped out of her coat. "I'm just in a weird mood."

"Do you want to talk about it?"

"No."

Noah nodded. "Okay. Do you want to fuck about it instead?"

Ashlyn laughed, leaning against him and wrapping her arms around his waist. "Sure. Maybe the endorphins will help."

"Come on." He scooped her up in a bridal carry and brought her to the living room.

She looped an arm around his neck, too drained to worry about being dropped. He sank down onto the couch, holding Ashlyn across his lap. Outside the big windows, his yard lights illuminated a winter wonderland of pine boughs heavy with snow. The potbellied stove in the corner crackled and snapped, radiating comforting heat.

Ashlyn yawned and snuggled into Noah. She felt the touch of his lips on the top of her head as her eyes slowly shuttered.

twenty-nine

AT SOME POINT in the night, Noah had carried Ashlyn upstairs to his bed. She woke in his arms, her face pressed into his chest, her legs tangled with his. The sun was about to rise, the eastern sky glowing behind the treetops, the light in the bedroom dim and gray. Noah's warm breath coasted over the top of her head, his body like a furnace against hers.

It felt so good and right and perfect, but last night's strange melancholy only deepened. Moving slowly, Ashlyn eased out of Noah's arms. She crept quietly downstairs, slipped into her coat and boots, and left.

She didn't know where she was going. She didn't know where she was supposed to go. She ended up, without meaning to, at her grandma's house. She parked at the curb and got out to stand on the front walk, staring up at the house again. The town was quiet. Snow fell in fat clumps, muting the quiet into utter silence.

Ashlyn wasn't sure how long she stood and stared at the house but, eventually, the sound of a panting dog, a jingling collar, and shuffling footsteps broke her out of whatever strange trance she was in. She turned—and immediately wished she hadn't.

"Mrs. Albrecht. Good morning. I'm surprised you're not at Mass."

"I go to the nine o'clock Mass," the old woman answered with a tone of affront. Her dog, a fluffy gray mop about the size of a football, strained at the leash, pulling towards Ashlyn.

"Oh. Well… have a nice day, then." Ashlyn started to turn away from her.

"Wait."

Ashlyn turned back, slightly dreading whatever was coming next.

"I apologize for some of the things I said to you. After we spoke last night, I had time to think. And it occurred to me that maybe Judy might have been as hard on her granddaughter as she was on herself. And the more I thought on it, I also realized that, regardless of my thoughts on the matter, it's not my place to decide who gets forgiveness and how they earn it." The words were delivered in a brittle, starchy tone that seemed at odds with an apology. It took a second for Ashlyn to realize she wasn't being scolded again.

"Oh, I, um— well, thank you for saying so."

Mrs. Albrecht nodded rigidly. "Have a good day, then."

"You, too." Ashlyn watched as she and her little dog made their way down the sidewalk. Some of the strange melancholy shifted, like a small weight being eased off.

Finding the motivation to move, she walked up to the front door and let herself inside. In the dim light, she could see the ghost of the old house laid over all of the changes. She blinked, and it was gone. But if she let her gaze soften just a little, it came back.

She walked through the house, keeping the ghost with her the entire time. The hallway, the living room, the kitchen, up the stairs in the bedrooms. She went back downstairs and stopped in front of the fireplace, staring at the empty space on the mantel where the wedding photo and Grandpa's ashes used to be. She could see them in her mind's eye like they were still there.

Her grandma had been a controlling, demeaning, cruel woman. But she'd suffered the same treatment from someone else. Maybe Ashlyn couldn't ever really forgive Judy Vandale for her mistreatment, but she could let go of the anger and pain. She didn't need it anymore.

"Goodbye, Grandma."

A quiet peace seemed to brush past her. The ghostly remnants of the old house faded away until she was standing only in the present.

She'd finally done what she set out to do.

She really wasn't going to get a better note to leave on, she realized with a grim sort of resignation. The house was done. She'd seen the Winter Market through to its opening, and any wrap-up work could be handled remotely. She could leave Noah without tears or painful goodbyes.

For the first time—and the last time—she could leave Lenora on a good note.

So why did she feel like crying?

She went back to her motel room, packed her things, and loaded them into her car. She felt weird taking the wedding photo and Grandpa's ashes back to Chicago, but she didn't know what else to do with them.

When everything was packed, she put her grandma's house keys in an envelope and gave them to the front desk clerk—Debbie's niece, Kiera.

"Give those to your Aunt Debbie for me?" Ashlyn asked, her throat uncomfortably tight.

Kiera promised she would, and then there was nothing left to keep her in Lenora. Noah flashed into her mind, but she quickly pushed him away. Her leave of absence couldn't last forever. And besides, Noah had told her he was up for a temporary fling. Permanence was not in the cards. Not for Ashlyn. Not in Lenora.

She finally got into her car. She looked around the familiar, comforting skyline of her tiny hometown as she pulled out. Her eyes burned, and she blinked hard as she drove. And then Lenora was in her rearview mirror. She couldn't fight it anymore—tears streaked her cheeks as she drove back to Chicago.

NOAH WOKE TO A QUIET HOUSE AND AN EMPTY BED, AND HE instantly *knew*. Ashlyn was gone. Not just gone from his house, but gone from Lenora and gone from his life. He lay in the cold stillness of his room for a while, willing himself to wake up into a different reality where Ashlyn was still here—one where she *stayed* here.

Eventually, he had to accept that he was awake and get out of bed. When he picked up his phone, he found a text message from Ashlyn.

Thank you. For everything.

He stared at the message until his screen darkened. There was a fist around his heart, squeezing, a band around his lungs, suffocating him. He'd known all along that this pain was coming. He'd let himself exist only in the present, ignoring it, and now it was here and he wasn't ready. He'd thought he had more time. She wasn't supposed to leave until after Christmas.

Still wearing yesterday's clothes, he got into his truck and drove over to Ashlyn's grandma's house, just to be sure. All the lights were out. There was a faint shadow of footprints in the snow leading up to the house. So she'd been here, but hours ago by the looks of it.

She was probably halfway back to Chicago by now.

The vice around his lungs squeezed tighter.

He kept on rolling past the house, into town. He had to divert around Main Street since it was closed to vehicles on the weekends for the market, taking him onto Lakeshore Drive. He pulled into the parking lot by the beach and turned the truck off. The lake was frozen over, though the ice wasn't yet thick enough for ice fishing. Snow covered it in a smooth velvety blanket.

Ashlyn would've liked it. She'd told him, multiple times, how the little inland lakes in the Northwoods were so different from the Great Lakes. How much more peaceful and quiet and cozy they felt. How there were no loons on Lake Michigan—at least, not down by Chicago. How you had to worry about rip tides and bacterial blooms if you swam in Lake Michigan.

Now she was headed back there, even though she obviously didn't love it the way she loved Lake Lenora. The way she loved the town, without even realizing it. The way she could've loved—

Well. Too late for that.

Noah got out of his truck and walked down to the shoreline. Lenora was a fifteen-hundred-acre lake with over seven miles of shoreline. He'd walked around it multiple times in his life. Always in the summer.

He glanced southward along the snowy shoreline. What else did he have to do with his day now that Ashlyn was gone? He started walking.

. . .

HE'D MADE IT NEARLY HALFWAY AROUND THE LAKE, TO THE southernmost point of Lake Lenora, by the town of Ellison —a place so tiny, it made Lenora look like a bustling metropolis. Ellison's beaches were less maintained than Lenora's, and smaller, with tall pine trees closing in tightly on either side of the small stretch of open shoreline. A few yards back from the water, a single car was parked in the parking lot. Noah glanced at it and kept walking before suddenly coming to a halt, staring back at the car.

It was a black Lexus, just like the one Ashlyn drove, with Illinois plates. He went over to it, trudging through deep snow. There was nobody inside, but he recognized the parking ramp sticker on the corner of her windshield. It was Ashlyn's car—or somebody who had the same car and used the same Chicago parking ramp on a regular basis.

Footprints in the snow led away from the car and into the cover of the trees. Noah followed them, his heart in his throat, barely able to breathe. A weird anxiety was coursing through him, equal parts anticipation and apprehension.

And then he saw her—a lone figure hunched over, sitting on a jutting granite boulder near the shoreline, but hidden within the cover of the trees. As he approached, she straightened and turned. She stared at him for what felt like forever, her eyes red and cheeks shiny with tears.

"Noah?"

"What are you doing here, Princess?"

ASHLYN DIDN'T KNOW WHAT TO SAY. SHE DIDN'T EVEN KNOW what she was feeling. How was she supposed to explain that she'd had to pull off the road because she couldn't see through her tears, and now she'd been sitting in the cold for nearly two hours, staring at the prettiest lake the in the world, trying to find the momentum necessary to leave? Apparently, the possibility of losing her career and everything she'd worked for wasn't a real strong motivator.

She opened her mouth, but she had no words. Nothing that would make any sense. Nothing that wasn't pathetic. She closed it.

Noah came closer. He sat on the cold granite next to her. "I was thinking," he said conversationally.

She wiped at her cheeks, waiting.

"You should stay in Lenora."

She blinked. "What?" her voice came out as a froggy rasp.

"You shouldn't go back to Chicago. You should stay in Lenora."

"I can't. My job—"

"Ash, I know you have a respectable position at a prestigious firm, but besides that, you don't seem to really care about your job that much. But you know what I've seen you throw yourself into? The Winter Market. Linda Moreau's salon. Jeremy Wagner's store. You could do all that up here. You could have your *own* firm." He paused. "Or could you? I'm actually not sure how that works in your field. But what I'm saying is, there's a place for you here. And I think you want to be here. I think you want to come back home."

Ashlyn choked on a snuffling sob. Just like that, the world flashed into technicolor possibility. *That*'s why she felt so miserable leaving Lenora—not because of her grandma's lingering presence, but because this was her home, and she didn't want to leave it again. The revelation was so painfully simple, her own obtuseness astounded her.

"Did I say the wrong thing? I'm sorry, Ash. Don't cry."

She took a minute to get her breath under control. "What about you?"

He blinked. "What about me?"

She took in a shaky breath, hugging her knees to her chest. "What would it mean to you if I stayed?"

"Ah." He was quiet for a second, and Ashlyn felt her stomach drop. "I told you I used to be obsessed with you." He said it carefully, thoughtfully. "To be honest, I don't think I ever stopped. You were gone for so long, it went dormant. But as soon as I saw you again—boom. Obsessed again." He paused. "Except I'm a grown man now, and calling it an 'obsession' sounds creepy."

Ashlyn snuffled on damp laughter.

"You told me you never felt like anybody's first choice. But, Princess, you would be mine. I've been half in love with you since we were kids, and seeing you again, knowing you again, tipped me all the way over. If you'd give me the chance, I'd spend every day making sure you felt it."

"Noah," Ashlyn sobbed, throwing herself at him. He caught her, hauling her into his arms and hugging her tightly to him. He kissed the top of her head, again and again, and when she lifted her tear-streaked face, he kissed her lips, her cheeks, her forehead.

Ashlyn reached up to cup his face with both hands, holding his gaze. "I've always been cautious and careful, but you make me feel reckless," she told him. "Reckless enough to kiss you when we were kids. Reckless enough to love you, now that we're grown."

"Ash," Noah said softly, dipping his head to kiss her again. "Thank god I can finally say it. I love you."

She was filled with an impossible contentment, a radiant glow that warmed her whole body, made her heart swell, made her cheeks hurt from smiling. "I love you, Noah." She buried her face in the crook of his neck, clinging to him, so happy she could scream from it.

"Princess, you're freezing. Why don't we get you back home?"

Home. Her home. Finally.

epilogue

"NOAH AND ASHLYN ARE HERE!" Renee Sorenson announced joyously to the packed house.

A few voices cheered in response—some sounded more sober than others. "Come in, come in!" She took the tray of mini quiches out of Ashlyn's hands. "You didn't have to make anything," she scolded. "But thank you, these smell amazing!"

"Thank you for having me again," Ashlyn said.

"She had no choice." Noah put his arm around Ashlyn's shoulders and pulled her into his side playfully.

Renee scoffed. "As if you have any say in the matter." She softened her words by pecking her son on the cheek. "But it makes invitations simpler now that she's your girl-friend." She smiled at both of them, obviously thrilled to bits. "Well, go on, take your coats off, get comfortable. I'm just going to take this to the kitchen." She swanned off with Ashlyn's tray.

"Ah, Noah." Wes appeared out of the mass of Sorensons like a handsome wraith. "I see you brought your not-girlfriend again."

"Haven't you heard the news?" Ashlyn asked. "I'm not his not-girlfriend anymore."

Wes took a second, obviously doing the math in his brain. He appeared to be slightly hindered by the nearly empty old fashioned in his hand. "So… you… *are* his girlfriend?"

"Good job, you got it." Noah patted his brother patronizingly on the shoulder.

"When did this happen?" Wes demanded, a slightly tipsy smile on his face.

"Well, officially, about three days ago."

"*Officially.*" Wes winked theatrically at them. "Gotcha."

Noah smiled uncertainly at his brother. "How many of those have you had?"

"This is lucky number five," Wes said, tipping it to his mouth and draining the last of it.

"Five is a lucky number?" Ashlyn asked.

"Maybe not. I should probably try six." Wes tilted his head, taking them both in. "I'm happy for you, Noah. And you should be happy for me."

Noah raised his brows. "Should I?"

"Yep—I figured out who owns the lake frontage from the old resort. And I figured out how to get it from him."

"Really? Are you serious?"

Wes tapped his finger against the side of his nose, then pointed intently at Noah. "It's a dowry."

"A… what?"

"Shhh." Wes looked around, then down at his empty glass. He seemed surprised to see it. "'Scuze me, I should probably go drink some water."

"I think that's a good idea," Noah said.

Wes ambled off, and Noah and Ashlyn exchanged puzzled looks.

"Is he alright?" Ashlyn asked.

"I'm not sure. I'll talk to him tomorrow, when he's sober."

"What's this I hear about a *girlfriend?*" A gray-haired, portly man with the characteristic Sorenson blue eyes clapped Noah on the back, grinning from beneath a thick gray mustache.

"Hey, Uncle Marty. This is Ashlyn. She was here at Thanksgiving."

"Oh, *right*, the girl you had your eye on. Finally snared her, hey?"

"Is that who this is?" Another old man demanded—this one with brown eyes, and threads of coal-black hair still running through all the gray.

"Uncle Louie, I don't know if you met Ashlyn? She's from Lenora originally, but she's been living in Chicago—"

Louie's bushy eyebrows shot up. "Oooh, I know this one. Judy Vandale's girl. The hotshot lawyer."

Ashlyn had never had to deal with jovial, slightly drunk uncles. She stood beside Noah, smiling weakly. "I'm a CPA, actually. But, yeah, that's me." For the first time, she didn't have to suppress a grimace at being identified by her relationship to her grandmother. For better or for worse (mostly for worse), Judy Vandale was a part of Ashlyn's past. And that past had brought her to this moment, arm in arm with Noah Sorenson, at a family Christmas party surrounded by loving, happy people.

"Well, that's even better. You file taxes?"

"Um, I mostly specialize in commercial clients, but—"

"Ashlyn's not doing your taxes," Noah told his uncle dryly.

"That's what family's for!" Louie objected, though there was a sly twinkle in his eye.

"She's not family, yet," Noah argued back.

Yet. The word struck Ashlyn like a gong. Not family *yet.*

She looked up at Noah, biting back a silly smile. He didn't seem to realize what he'd said. He was caught in a heated, but toothless debate with his uncle.

"—helped you with that downed tree, didn't I?"

"Because you wanted the wood for your fireplace!"

"How'd my sweet little nephew become so cynical? What is the world coming to when a man can't—"

"Lou, stop harassing my son," Renee said, appearing out of nowhere with a pot of coffee in one hand and an oven mitt on the other. "Mary's looking for you. Says you're not wearing the sweater she made you."

Louie cursed under his breath. "Don't let that woman find me."

"You're hiding from your own sister?"

"Just one of them."

"Some family man," Renee scoffed.

While Louie spluttered his defense, Noah nudged Ashlyn and nodded towards the kitchen. Feeling slightly rude about it, she followed Noah, slipping away from his mother and uncles.

"If Uncle Louie traps you in a conversation, you'll have to fake your own death to escape," Noah explained quietly while he examined all the snacks and hors d'oeuvres. "Mom periodically runs interference if she sees he's cornered someone for too long."

"Your mom might be an actual angel."

"You haven't seen her when she catches someone with their shoes on in the house." Noah picked up a plate and began filling it with snacks.

"Oh-ho! And who's this?"

Another aunt and uncle, then a couple of cousins were introduced. As Noah and Ashlyn threaded their way back to the gaming room, they bumped into Aiden as he was slinking away from the chaos, then Lucas and Rowan who were arguing with two younger cousins about the rules of thumb wars.

"James isn't here?" Ashlyn asked. He'd been notably absent at Thanksgiving as well.

"Yeah. James lives in Minneapolis and usually goes to his wife's family for holidays. We don't see him too often these days." Noah said it casually, but there was a thread of resentment Ashlyn couldn't help but pick up on.

"Do you miss him?"

"Yeah." Noah sighed. "Anyway—" he nudged the door to the game room open "—time to kick some ass. What're we playing?"

"Ashlyn!" Jenny cried happily from the card table. "You made it!"

"*I'm* here too," Noah pointed out.

"Yeah, but you were a given." Jenny pointed to the empty seats. "Sit down, we'll deal you guys in."

"Jenny never got her revenge," Ashlyn said suddenly as they were driving home.

Ostensibly, they had separate homes—Ashlyn was technically renting the Hendrix cottage out on Townline Road. In actual practice, Ashlyn had never even slept one night there. She had most of her toiletries in his bathroom. Half of his dresser drawers were filled with her clothes. But, most importantly, every night she slept in his bed. Every day she made noise about "moving too fast" and needing to be "practical" but every night she ended up with him, where she belonged.

"Revenge?" Noah asked, bemused.

"She vowed revenge on me at Thanksgiving for the potato salad trick. I waited all night for her to try something, but she never did. Do you think she's saving it for some other time? Waiting until my guard is down?"

"Maybe her revenge is making you wonder about it forever."

Ashlyn was quiet for a moment. "That would be evil. And genius."

They drove in silence for a few minutes, when something suddenly occurred to Noah. "Oh, hey, I ran into Janice Albrecht at the grocery store. She told me to tell you that she—and I quote—'dumped him in the burn barrel.'"

Ashlyn's smile had a worrying degree of malice in it.

"Do I want to know?"

"Probably not."

"Should I at least have an alibi prepared for you?"

She laughed. "I didn't know what to do with my grandpa's ashes, so I gave them to Mrs. Albrecht and asked her to figure it out since she's involved with the church and everything. I wasn't expecting this solution, but I suppose it's fitting."

"I thought she was your grandma's best friend?"

Ashlyn nodded, turning her gaze out the window. "She was."

There was a world of secret meaning in that brief sentence, but he sensed Ashlyn wasn't ready to talk about it, so he left it alone.

Back at the house, they went to the living room to sit in the cozy glow of the Christmas tree.

"Do you want your Christmas present?" Noah asked. He'd been impatient to give it to her since he'd gotten it.

"It's not Christmas yet."

"Lots of people open gifts on Christmas Eve."

"Does your family?"

He let out a frustrated breath. "No."

She laughed. "Alright, let's start our own tradition, then."

He sprang off the couch and plucked up two wrapped boxes from under the tree—one large, one small. Ashlyn retrieved a single oblong one and rejoined him on the couch.

"You first." Noah shoved his gifts into her hands.

She started with the larger and much heavier of the two, peeling the paper back to reveal a kit of bread-making tools —a bench scraper, a brotform, a razor lame, a sourdough crock, a baker's couche, and a rectangular baking stone.

"You said you like baking bread, even though you didn't have much time for it. Hopefully, now that you're your own boss with smaller-scale clients, you can find the time to make bread."

She blinked in a way that looked suspiciously like trying not to cry. "Noah, thank you so much! This is so sweet!"

"Open the other one," he prompted.

The tiny one was a velvet jewelry box. She cast a dubious look at him.

"Open it," he prompted.

She lifted the hinged lid. Set in the pillowed crease was an ordinary steel key. She frowned at it. "This is—?"

"Your own house key. I know you're renting your own place, and I'm not asking you to give it up. But I want you to come and go from here as you please. Treat it like your own house, Ash. Decorate, if you want. Put your stuff wherever. Stay in bed when I have to be up early and you don't. Chill here even if I'm not home. Just... it's yours."

"Noah," she said softly, losing the fight against tears. A single one tracked down her cheek and she swiped it away. "Thank you," she said, voice thick with feeling.

"It's not too fast?"

She let out a soft, laughing breath. "I think we've established that I'm a reckless fool when it comes to you. Why try to change now?"

"Good call." He leaned in and kissed her.

"Okay, now you." She pressed her gift into his hands.

He unwrapped it slowly, wondering what it could be. "A propane camp stove?" he asked, looking at the box. Was this her way of saying she wanted to go camping?

"No, that's just the box I used. Open it."

He peeled the cardboard flaps open and laughed in disbelief. "*Ashlyn*. A skateboard?"

"You were having so much fun that day at the park. And I always loved watching you skate. And it seems like all you do is work, and you need something fun and relaxing." She smiled uncertainly. "Is it too much? I have the receipt. I can return it."

"No, this is amazing. I can't believe... wait, did you say you 'always loved watching me skate'?"

Her cheeks colored slightly. "Yes. I used to creep on you from behind the bleachers after soccer practice."

"*What?* For how long?"

"Basically all four years of high school during soccer season."

He stared at her. "Ashlyn, if they ever invent time travel, I'm going back to our freshman year to beat some sense into myself."

She laughed and leaned into him, wrapping her arms

around his waist. "No time traveling! It's too dangerous. What if you create a rip in the time-space continuum and then I never see you again?"

He sighed. "You're right. It's too risky."

She sighed, her head resting against his chest. "I love you, Noah. Merry Christmas."

He bent to kiss the top of her head. "Merry Christmas, Princess. I love you."

thank you

Thank you for reading *What Could Have Been!* If you enjoyed it (or even if you didn't), please consider reviewing or recommending it on social media and/or the retailer where you purchased it. Word of mouth has a huge impact on an author's success, and it helps other readers find new books to enjoy.

If you want to be alerted to my new releases, as well as receive exclusive bonus content (including bonus epilogues and deleted scenes) you can ***subscribe to my newsletter***.

also by heather guerre

Preferential Treatment

Contemporary romance

———

Tooth & Claw **series:**

Paranormal Shifter and Vampire Romances

Cold Hearted

Hot Blooded

Once Bitten

———

Hellbound **series:**

Paranormal Demon Romances

Demon Lover

about the author

Heather Guerre writes sexy-sweet fantasy, sci-fi, and contemporary romances. A hopeless romantic and an unapologetic nerd, Heather loves everything to do with romance, aliens, shifters, cyborgs, monsters, and magic.

For more from Heather, you can subscribe to her newsletter at heatherguerre.com/newsletter. Subscribers receive alerts for new releases as well as newsletter-exclusive bonus material.

❄

Made in the USA
Las Vegas, NV
10 December 2022

61722812R00135